T0129546

In Search of Cloud People

Also by Dennis McKay

Novels:
Fallow's Field (2007)
Once Upon Wisconsin (2009)
A Boy Fom Bethesda (2013)
The Shaman and the Stranger (2015)
The Accidental Philanderer (2015)
A Girl From Bethesda (2017)
Summer of Tess (2018)
Bethany Blue (2019)

Nonfiction:
Terrapin Tales, with coauthor Scott McBrien (2016)

Book cover design by Megan Clifford.

In Search of Cloud People

Dennis McKay

IN SEARCH OF CLOUD PEOPLE

iUniverse books may be ordered through booksellers or by contacting:

iUniverse
1663 Liberty Drive
Bloomington, IN 47403
www.iuniverse.com
1-800-Authors (1-800-288-4677)

ISBN: 978-1-5320-9184-1 (sc)
ISBN: 978-1-5320-9185-8 (e)

Library of Congress Control Number: 2019921179

Print information available on the last page.

iUniverse rev. date: 01/09/2020

Prologue

1999

The world as Yachay knew it was in turmoil. Yesterday on his trek up the mountain, dark, billowy clouds had lifted from the horizon, shrouding the sky in misty gloom. With the clouds came the strong and unmistakable scent of snow; soon enough, chaotic gusts of swirling wind—snow devils—preceded a furious, growling storm of thunder and snow. After an unsettling lull, it would rage yet again.

Yachay had sought shelter three times before reaching his mountainside abode at dusk, when at last the storm relented. In all his forty-four years living on the mountain, he had never experienced such weather. Something to do with the *yuraq ghari* (white man) and his guide, Aldo?

At the ancient ruins of sacrifice, Yachay had shared a meal with them on their journey up the mountain to his birth village, Olaquecha, and the shaman. Yachay felt an immediate bond with both men but especially with the white man, Pedro, who was on a *nuna puriy* (spirit journey) to heal a terminal illness. He had a gritty determination and resilient spirit that Yachay found compelling. Though uncertain as to how the shaman would greet a stranger—a white man no less—Yachay had intuited an aura of destiny, as though Pedro had been anointed with a current of vitality from some distant past.

After awakening this morning, Yachay could tell by the arrangement of things in the mountainside abode—chairs not all the way tucked under the table, the pottery cups not bottom-side up on the shelf—that they had recently stopped here on their way down the mountain.

Yachay shifted his attention to the russet-gold rays of the sun that were lifting between the snowcapped mountains shimmering in the distance. It was a sight he never grew tired of. These mountains were his home, his sanctuary, where he answered to no man and was free to roam and exist as he pleased.

Turning back toward his mountainside abode, Yachay caught a glimpse of a black speck high overhead. As it came closer, he recognized *el condor*, soaring in a circle, its great wings gliding with the currents. A sudden awareness came over Yachay. *Pedro and Aldo are in trouble. Big trouble.* There was no time to waste.

After storing jerky and raw quinoa in his burlap waist bag, and filling his bota bag with water, Yachay went to the corral, past the four llamas—they looked fine. They were self-sufficient animals as long as they had grass or grain and water in the trough. The billy and nanny goats also managed on their own.

From under the lean-to, Yachay retrieved the travois, a platform of leather netting mounted on two long poles, supported by cross braces, lashed together in the shape of a triangle. The travois was a light but effective means to transport a heavy weight by either one or two men attached to a leather harness.

Yachay figured Aldo and Pedro would take the same route down the mountain that he had given them for the way up. He secured a harness to his shoulders and set out around the llama corral and then through the long and wide, snow-covered meadow, which yesterday morning had been alive with perennial grasses, sedges, and wildflowers. Only the Puyas stood above the blanket of snow, their foliage of long and sharp leaves spiraling like sentinel obelisks.

Through a rocky-wall opening, he came to Qhusi Qucha, an aqua-blue tarn. Yachay looked for any indication that they had been there. No footprints and no yellow snow, but that was not unusual on this mountain. The wind and snow could cover any trace of living things in little time.

By midmorning, Yachay was halfway down the second of four switchbacks when he came to a ledge abutting the mountainside. Overhead, crevices and juts in the rock provided a foothold to access a small cave that he used for shelter. "Pedro ... Aldo!" Yachay yelled up to the cave entrance.

Silence.

Yachay looked for any sign. At the back of the ledge was a backpack. He shimmied up the ledge and inspected the contents of the pack: lightweight hiking pants, two pairs of socks, undergarments, and a tightly knitted gray sweater shirt that Yachay recognized as Pedro's.

Had Pedro fallen and injured himself trying to reach the cave? Where was Aldo's backpack? Did they get separated?

Yachay secured the backpack on the travois and continued down the trail, the mountain on his right, the valley to his left. Around a bend, he saw a motionless figure sitting with his back to a ledge, legs splayed out, facing the valley. It was Pedro, but what a sight he was. His face was a sickly faded blue, his eyebrows and chin covered in a layer of ice, and there was a dark-purple bruise on his cheek. Yachay wasn't sure if he was dead or alive. He put his index and middle finger on the side of Pedro's neck. There was a pulse, a weak one, but he was alive.

Yachay turned the travois around, put his hands under Pedro's armpits, and maneuvered him onto the platform. He tied him to the travois with straps around his chest and thighs. He hoped Aldo had found shelter, but he sensed the worse for the guide, for he would not have left Pedro alone. Yachay feared for Aldo's well-being, but he had no choice other than to get Pedro to the mountainside abode.

This was the first time Yachay had pulled a person in the travois other than a dry run with Tian. He stopped three times to rest and check Pedro's pulse, relieved each time to find a heartbeat. When he reached level ground at the end of the last switchback, the muscles in his shoulders and arms were burning with fatigue.

After a respite, Yachay continued on, passing around the aqua-blue tarn and then the slow and cumbersome work of weaving his way through the stony terrain of the rocky-wall opening.

By late afternoon, Yachay pulled into the meadow, the mountainside abode now in sight, his body exhausted from the effort.

Yachay pushed the heavy wooden door open and dragged the travois into his dwelling—a natural cavity in the side of the mountain—which offered immediate warmth from the brisk air.

In the middle of the space was a table made of logs roughly mortised and tenoned together, with two chairs made of wood and vines. The floor was hard-packed earth, and the mostly stone walls were braced by wood studs where needed. On one side of the space were two woven reed mats, each with a blanket rolled up at the top. On the other side was a flat stone the size and shape of a small, round tabletop, which was used for preparing food. Behind the stone were three burlap sacks filled with grain and dry goods; above the dry goods was a rough-hewn shelf, running the length of the wall, with wooden utensils and cups, pots, and plates made of earthenware.

Yachay checked Pedro's pulse—still weak.

After getting Pedro onto a mat and covered in a blanket, Yachay removed Pedro's boots and socks and noticed one of his ankles was swollen and bruised a deep blue and purple. He rubbed Pedro's feet—which were ice cold—vigorously, first one and then the other. Yachay put dry socks, from Pedro's backpack, on him and then wrapped his feet and legs snugly with the blanket.

Yachay dapped a cloth in a bowl of water and wiped the remaining bits of ice from Pedro's eyebrows and chin. His face, no longer blue, was regaining the ruddy color of good health that Yachay had noticed the first time he had met Pedro—a handsome, regal-looking man with high cheekbones, a square jaw, and a full head of dark-brown hair with wisps of gray on the side.

How he had survived in that storm last night was a mystery, but here he was alive.

Yachay left Pedro and went outside to the pile of dried llama dung and then over to the firepit. After starting the dung fire with flint and stone, he checked on Pedro, who was still unconscious. From the shelf, he removed a pitcher of water, a clay pot, and a bowl of dried coca leaves.

After the fire died down, Yachay placed the pot, filled with the water and coca leaves, over red coals.

Back in the hut, Yachay poured the steaming tea into a cup.

He crouched down next to Pedro, dipped a cloth in the tea, and lightly ran the cloth over his lips. He continued to do this, patiently moistening his lips, until Pedro's eyes flickered as though trying to open.

"Pedro," Yachay said.

Pedro's eyes opened, and his mouth gaped askew with a look of shock and bewilderment. He gasped. "No. Aldo. No!"

Yachay asked, "Aldo, kay icha aya?" (Aldo, alive or dead?)

Pedro squinted as though trying to understand the question. He then shook his head, his eyes blinking slowly. "Dead," he said before his eyes closed.

CHAPTER

1

2007
Portland, Oregon

I t had been eight years since Devon's father, Peter Richards, had left for Peru in search of a shaman and a cure for terminal brain cancer. After two weeks had passed with no word from Peter, Debra Richards phoned the American embassy in Lima in regard to her missing husband. The embassy then contacted the office of the guide who was to escort Peter Richards up a mountain in a remote part of northern Peru, but Peter and his guide, Aldo Coreas, never returned.

A search party was sent out, and the body of Coreas was found at the bottom of a gorge, but there was no sign of Peter Richards. The village of Olaquecha that Peter had been searching for was wrapped in myth. Most people did not believe in its existence, and those who did said it was a dangerous, difficult journey. A staff member at the embassy told Debra that they had to conclude that her husband was dead.

A series of events had led Peter Richards to travel to South America in search of a shaman and a miracle. Months before his terminal diagnosis, Peter had sunk into a deep and sullen depression. He had little interest in work, his family, or even his lifetime passion, stargazing.

1

After his diagnosis, a visit to a cancer clinic only darkened his mood. "I would be going there to die," Devon overheard his father say to his mother when he returned from the clinic.

Peter told Debra that he had recently found out about a high school friend who lost his battle with cancer. "I called his wife to offer belated condolences," Peter said. "Toward the end, she said he was an unrecognizable skeleton, having lost seventy pounds before finally and mercifully dying. *Grueling* was the word she used to describe it. I don't want you and Devon to have to go through that."

Then there was a radio show Peter had listened to in his car, where a man who had been given a year to live went to the Andes and was healed by a shaman. "This guy sounded like a no-BS straight shooter," Peter mentioned at the dinner table, one of the few times in months he had initiated a conversation.

But Devon and his mother never took any of these musings seriously. In hindsight, it seemed so desperate and unlike his father. Devon now wondered if it was a side effect from the cancer—mental instability. His father had always been a firm believer in natural science.

The clincher was when Bob Goodman, the family physician, arranged a meeting between Peter and an archaeologist who had been doing research in Peru for years. Dr. Neil Judd told Peter that he had seen things over the years that made him a believer in the healing abilities of shamans.

Then came the family meeting at the kitchen table. Peter said to his wife and son, "In regard to my cancer, I have decided to go to Lima, Peru, hire a guide, and seek a cure from a shaman residing in a mountain village in the Andes."

"Dad, a shaman in Peru, in South America?" Devon said with edgy disbelief.

"Peter, a mountain village? I never thought you were really serious about all this." Debra looked at her husband as if he had lost his mind. "How in your condition are you going to do this?"

"I still have my physical abilities." Peter fixed his eyes on the floor for a moment. When he looked up, there was a terrible tension around his eyes. "I know this must sound crazy to the both of you, but what have I got to lose?" Peter looked at his wife, his dark eyes so desperately determined. It was a look Devon had never seen before from his father. "I can stay here and die—a horrible death, according to Bob Goodman—or I can, for once in my life, take a chance on a miracle."

"Peter," Debra said, "please reconsider."

"What is there to reconsider?" Peter said with a quiver of impatience. He reached for Debra's hand, but she pulled it away.

"What about *us*, Peter?" Debra then glanced toward Devon, who remembered the shock of it all, as he sat with his mouth open in a little circle, trying to comprehend what was occurring.

"Is it fair that you're running away from us?" Debra looked at Peter as if searching for a trace of the pragmatic man she had married. "When you have so little time?"

A silent pause hung in the air.

"I have made my decision."

"Wow." Debra let out a stream of air like an empty whistle. She glanced at a stunned Devon and back at Peter, her expression deflating from upset to hurt. "When are you departing, Peter?" Debra's voice was thin, scarcely a thread of sound. It was a voice of surrender.

"I plan on leaving the day after tomorrow."

Debra dropped her gaze, emitting a low grunt. "Dear God," she said.

Devon screeched his chair back from the table, knocking it over, and stood. "It's not fair. How come Mom and I don't have a say in this?"

"No, Dev, it's not fair, but that's the way it is." Peter looked at the fallen chair and then back at his son. "So let's try and make the best of it."

Devon had read of a Japanese soldier from World War II having survived in a Philippines jungle for nearly thirty years. Could his father have been healed by the shaman and still be alive on a remote mountain in Peru, unable for some reason to return home?

He wasn't sure where his mother stood on the possibility of his father surviving. She never talked about it, though she never removed her wedding band. After a period of mourning, Debra Richards went on with her life: maintaining the raised garden beds—assembled by Peter with slots and pegs—she and her husband had tended to in the backyard every year, socializing with the wives of her husband's business partners at Ebert, Heiden & Richards Architects, and volunteering three days a week at the Red Cross.

Devon was fourteen when he last saw his father, and for the last eight years, he had continued on through high school, then on to the University of California at Berkley, where he had recently graduated with a degree in structural engineering and a minor in astronomy. During college, Devon had looked into shamanism online, but his education as an applied science major kept telling him it was hocus-pocus, nothing more. But there was an inexplicable nagging sense to not give up hope, a sense that went against everything he had learned in college.

Back home from school, Devon couldn't get serious about a job search—not until he learned more about his father's disappearance. He called the family physician, Dr. Goodman, who was someone Devon trusted for advice, and arranged a meeting at his office for the following day. "To discuss my father … and," he said with a trace of uncertainty in his voice, "a personal matter."

Devon sat across a double-pedestal mahogany desk from Dr. Goodman at his medical office. Pictures of Bob Goodman and his wife in exotic locales hung on the wall behind him. Below each photograph was a brief description: Aoraki Mount Cook, New Zealand. Shamwari Game Reserve, South Africa. Taj Mahal, India. In each photo, Bob Goodman's expression was not that of a tourist but a confident man immersed in the culture, the gaze steady and sure, shoulders straight, and a toothy smile of one on a great adventure.

"So, what brings you here, Devon?" Dr. Goodman asked.

"Ever since my father left …" Devon shrugged and continued, "I've had these overwhelming feelings that he survived. Not a vision but more an awareness, in a place, or more specifically a mental space, that I cannot put a name to."

Devon arched a brow as if to say, *Are you with me?*

The doctor nodded for him to continue.

"I've kept this to myself, not sure what to make of it. During high school and when home from college, it occurs on the observation platform in our backyard that he built by himself for stargazing, and always when I am alone at night, a sense that my father is alive."

They exchanged a look for a beat.

Devon raised his hands, palms up, and made a face to indicate it was out of his control. "Everything I have learned in school is based on scientific facts. These feelings I get about my dad are … I had an astronomy professor," Devon said in a voice raw with conflict, "who said, and I quote, 'There is no such thing as the supernatural.'" Devon looked at Bob for a reaction.

"What do you think, Devon?"

"Well," he said, "for my father to be alive, it would be to my advantage to believe in the supernatural."

Devon stared into his hands for a moment. "It's an *overwhelming* sense that he is alive—and *always* on the observation deck, as though there is a residue of his essence still there."

Devon shook his head. "I can't explain it, Dr. Goodman, but …"

"Devon," Dr. Goodman said as his eyes, dark blue and heavy lidded, slanted a look at Devon, "there's a quote from *Hamlet* that

5

sums up what I believe: 'There are more things in heaven and earth, Horatio, than are dreamt of in your philosophy.'"

"So you think—"

Dr. Goodman cut in, "Before we proceed any further, there's someone I would like you to meet."

CHAPTER

2

G ales Creek was a rural community forty-five minutes northwest of Portland. During the summer of Devon's twelfth year, he and his father had camped out in Gale Creek Campground. Located in Tillamook Forest, it had been a great adventure with hiking, swimming, fishing, and, of course, stargazing at night. Before Peter's illness, he had promised Devon they would return.

Down an old country lane, Bob pointed to a property nestled in a grove of shade trees. "Here we are—Dr. Judd's home, Devon," he said as he pulled into the gravel driveway. The grassless front yard was dotted with shrubs and bushes and patches of moss, ivy, and pachysandra.

On the drive over, Bob had told Devon that Neil Judd had worked for National Geographic, doing archeological research on various Indian tribes in the American Southwest, Central America, and South America.

Devon remembered how impressed his father had been after meeting with Dr. Judd. "That man is the real deal—a man of science who has been influenced by experiences in faraway lands." It was the first time in months his father had a semblance of his old spark back.

Neil Judd's home was a Spanish colonial style: low terra-cotta clay roof, stucco walls, and double-hung sash windows with carved wooden brackets and balustrades. From the driveway, a flagstone walk led to an adobe brick courtyard with stone benches. The front door was set back by an entryway with an arched opening built of granite stones.

Devon and Dr. Goodman were greeted at the front door by a gentleman in his late seventies, with receding gray hair combed straight back, accentuating a high forehead and a long, friendly face.

Dr. Neil Judd wore a tweed jacket with patches at the elbows and a leather string tie clipped to a white shirt by a silver clasp pitted with bits of turquoise. He reminded Devon of an older version of one of his astronomy professors—a man with an intellectual bearing and an aura of quiet certitude.

Beyond the dimly lit foyer, two steps rose into the living room, well lit by a massive skylight. Indian artifacts hung on the walls—a handcrafted bow, crossed arrows with colorful stone arrowheads, feather art, and a willow hoop dream catcher. Occupying the middle of the hardwood floor was a rectangular-shaped, handwoven rug with a zigzag border in gray and black and four colorful squares in the corners, each with a half man, half bird wearing a headdress. The man and his house gave Devon the sense that he had come to the right place.

The rear of the living room flowed into a dining nook, which opened to the kitchen, where a dark-haired woman stood with her back to them. She was preparing something that Devon couldn't make out.

They sat in high-arched chairs around a coffee table centered on the handwoven rug. "Vilma," Dr. Judd said over his shoulder toward the kitchen, "we are ready for *chicha.*"

"One moment please," she said with her back still turned. Her voice had a faint echo of south of the border.

Neil turned his attention back to his guests. "Do you know that Vilma's nephew, Rudy Arredondo, is a guide based in Lima?" He raised his brow as though he had intuited secret information. "He was a member of the search party—"

Vilma came into the room holding a tray balancing three cups and a clay teapot with brightly colored, overlapping V-shaped patterns. She was a beautiful and shapely woman, dressed in a lavender cotton skirt and a sleeveless blouse, her supple arms hinting at feminine strength.

She offered a shy smile that revealed a row of even white teeth. She might have been forty or fifty. It was difficult to say, for there were few wrinkles on her smooth, olive-skinned face. Her large brown eyes took in Devon and Bob as she placed the tray on an end table next to Dr. Judd's chair.

"Bob," Dr. Judd said, "you remember my wife, Vilma."

"Of course. Vilma, good to see you again," he said with a gentlemanly nod. "May I introduce Devon Richards."

"Hallo, Devon," Vilma said, her accent now most pronounced.

As Vilma returned to the kitchen, Neil Judd began pouring the tea. "Chicha is Quechua tea made of cornmeal," he said as he handed Bob a cup of tea.

"Vilma," Dr. Judd said with a half look over his shoulder, "was my best discovery in all my years in Peru." He then shifted himself in his seat and said as though mostly to himself, "Where was I?" He raised a finger. "Ah, yes. Rudy Arredondo."

"Tell us about him," Bob said as he tasted his tea and nodded his approval.

"Actually," Dr. Judd said with a knowing lift of the brow, "twenty years' experience ..." He paused in midsentence, poured a tea, and handed it to Devon. "He was a good friend of your father's guide in search of Olaquecha and the shaman there. He was the one who first discovered the body of Aldo Coreas."

"Really?" Devon said after tasting his tea. It was thin bodied and harshly sweet but not bad. "Yes, the body of Coreas was recovered but not my father's." Devon shifted in his chair, placed his teacup on the coffee table, and leaned forward, eyes on Dr. Judd. "Is there any chance that Olaquecha exists? And if so, could my father still be alive?"

He threw his hands out in front of himself. "Or is this totally crazy?" Devon squinted a look to indicate, *Tell me I am not nuts.*

"The village of Olaquecha is purported to be high in the most remote part of an isolated mountain in northern Peru and was first talked about in Western civilization little more than fifty years ago."

Dr. Judd took a slow, steady sip of his tea and then said, "Occasionally, there were rumors of some miracle healing, but never was there corroboration, and as time went by, few believed them real."

Neil Judd gave his brow a scratch and said, "So there it stayed, a myth, until a colleague had contact with a man who claimed to have proof."

"Did he have real proof?" Devon asked.

"Ah yes, the rub. An Indian native who made his living as a mountain porter was found north of Trujillo, wandering the highway, delirious and suffering from frostbite."

Vilma interrupted, asking Neil if they needed anything else before she went out. "No thank you, my dear," Neil said as his eyes followed Vilma down the step into the foyer and out the front door.

He continued, "He was rushed to the hospital. During his convalescence, he claimed to have been the only survivor of a group from his village who trekked Olaquecha Mountain seeking various cures from the shaman. My colleague got wind of this and went to the hospital."

Neil topped off his teacup and said, "I know it sounds like some wild story." He took long sip of his tea and smacked his lips in a silent *ah.* "But," he said to Devon, "there was physical proof. The man had been blind in one eye since childhood from a virus. There was a doctor who tended to the porter's village and verified the blindness."

Devon's mouth felt suddenly dry. He took a gulp of his tea, not tasting it, as his mind was racing. After exchanging a look with Bob, Devon turned his attention back to Dr. Judd.

"The porter claimed his vision was restored by the shaman," Neil Judd said in a matter-of-fact voice. "They ran some tests and discovered his vision was twenty-twenty in both eyes."

"What happened to this porter?" Devon asked.

"This is where it gets interesting," Dr. Judd said as he placed his cup on the table and squinted a look at Devon. "He disappeared from the hospital, never to be seen again." Dr. Judd gestured to Bob. "I have documents on this if you care to look them over."

Devon glanced at Bob, as if to say, *Do you believe this?*

"Neil," Dr. Goodman said, "has anyone tried to return to Olaquecha?"

"My colleague tried, but the weather didn't cooperate—snow squalls, high winds. They abandoned the mission."

"Has anyone returned?" Devon said.

"No. You know how these things are." Dr. Judd lifted his cup and stared into it for a moment and then said, "People have inspiration for a time. Then it passes, and other things draw their attention." He took a long swallow of his chicha, finishing it. "After a while, it only adds credence to the myth."

Dr. Judd straightened in his chair and raised his index finger. "What I can tell you is that shamans have great power—especially in their realm." He looked at Devon, as though to say, *Are you with me?*

"If your father made it to the shaman, there is a chance he was cured." Neil Judd shifted his gaze to Dr. Goodman. "Of course, there is a much greater chance that he perished."

"Neil," Bob said, "what Devon and I are looking for are answers." Bob lifted a finger as though to make a point. "Why didn't the search party find Peter Richards?" Bob sipped his tea and grimaced a swallow. "We would like resolution—whether somehow Peter is alive, or at the very least to find out what happened to him."

"I have some documents to give you on Olaquecha," Neil said through an emerging smile. "To paraphrase Churchill, 'it is a riddle wrapped inside an enigma.' Indian lore says it is the land of Cloud People." Neil lifted his brow, accentuating the age lines on his

11

forehead. "I believe it is a worthy journey to go in search of Cloud People."

◎

As they headed for Bob Goodman's car, Devon stopped on the flagstone path and said, "Dr. Goodman, I think I need to go to Peru."

Dr. Goodman nodded before a grin emerged in the corner of his mouth. "If you give me a couple of weeks to clear things up at my practice, I will join you."

After Dr. Goodman dropped off Devon, he stood on the front stoop, trying to find the appropriate words to tell his mother about what he had decided. He thought of the worried look on her face when she had discovered him in his father's home office last week, with his laptop showing a picture of a man in a colorful knitted cap and matching shawl, backdropped by mountains. Written in bold letters was "Welcome to Peru Shamans."

"What are you doing, Dev?" Debra's voice had a querulous tremor to it that Devon hadn't heard since the last family meeting before his father departed for Peru.

"Looking into shamans, Mom." Devon made an *I can't help myself* face.

"Devon?" Debra said in a ratcheted-up tone, the tone of a concerned mother.

"Mom," Devon said, "I'm just looking."

They had looked at each other for a beat, and in that moment, a look of realization came over Debra.

Devon found his mother sitting at the kitchen table as though she knew what was coming. "I saw Dr. Goodman drop you off, Devon. What's going on?"

Devon stood behind a chair, his hands gripping the top rail. "Dr. Goodman and I have decided to go to Peru to try to find out what happened to Dad."

Debra covered her face with her hands and said, "Dear God. Dear, dear *God.*"

Devon pulled back the chair, sat next to his mother, and reached for her hand.

Debra squeezed Devon's hand and said in a firm voice, "Devon, don't you think if your father were alive, he would have returned home by now?"

"Maybe he can't, Mom." Devon laced his fingers through his mother's and said, "That's why I have to go. To find out for sure."

"Are you going to climb that godforsaken mountain?"

CHAPTER

3

B ob Goodman had never been to Peru—or South America, for that matter; the closest he had been was a medical conference in Belize. Like all his other travels around the world, Bob did extensive research on Peru and the little he could find on the mountain village of Olaquecha. He found it incredulous that in the twenty-first century, there could be a Shangri-la hidden away from civilization in a remote section of the northern Andes.

In his research, Bob learned that the Quechua culture was old—a thousand years older than the Inca Empire. It was a culture with fascinating spiritual beliefs wrapped in myths of supernatural events. Shamans, who were big medicine in Quechua culture, acted as intermediaries between the temporal and spiritual realms and possessed a strong tradition of herbal medicine.

But most of the anthropology and archaeology experts considered the village of Olaquecha a myth.

At sixty-six years old, Bob Goodman had lived enough and seen enough things in faraway lands to keep an open mind about Olaquecha existing, but even if it did, could Peter really have survived? Bob wondered if, possibly, Peter had been healed, and on the way down the mountain, he'd witnessed his guide's demise and then decided to return to the village. It was a long shot—a big long shot—but Bob felt responsible for Peter embarking on his journey for a miracle cure, since he had encouraged him to consider going—not telling him to specifically go but confirming that staying meant a certain agonizing death.

◎

After seeing his last and final patient until his return from Peru, Bob Goodman called Devon to go over last-minute details. After going over Bob's checklist of items to bring—all of which Devon had already packed—Devon said, "I'm good to go, Dr. Goodman, but my mother is a wreck."

Bob had received a phone call from Debra a few days ago, and Devon was right. She was a wreck. "I have already lost Devon's father to that godforsaken land … and now Devon …" Her voice trailed off, and Bob could feel her anguish mounting. He had tried to reassure her but to little avail.

"Is your mother at home?"

"Yes," Devon said with a lift in his voice.

"Tell her I'll be over in half an hour."

Hemlock Hills was a brand-new neighborhood when Peter and Debra Richards purchased their house, which Peter had designed to the last detail, with Debra's input. Bob had been their family physician since they had moved in, around the time Devon was born. Bob and Peter hit it off right from the start, and Bob even ran a few half marathons with Peter until Bob's body told him biking and hiking might be more suitable on his joints.

Bob drove through the brick-walled entrance to Hemlock Hills. Ever since Peter's diagnosis, the irony of the name and Peter's situation was a quirk of fate that Bob had kept to himself.

The brickwork was for decorative purposes only, a welcoming construct of eight-foot-high walls of alternating stretching and heading courses of red colonial brick, extending twenty feet on each side.

Prior to the wall's construction, Peter had told Bob that he had gotten hold of a copy of the blueprints and took issue with the utilitarian twin-walled design. He offered to design gratis a protruding and recessed, two-way arched brick entrance with stone pilasters, but the developer wouldn't go for it. Rectangles and straight lines were never Peter's cup of tea, preferring arches and irregularity in form.

But after the wall was built, English ivy was planted at the base and soon covered both columns and walls, making moot his more elaborate design. Peter told Bob he was fine with it. "I admire ivy's dark-green beauty, and it's such a resilient, hardy plant that has the survival instincts that I admire."

Past the entrance, Bob accelerated into the community of the neo-craftsman bungalows and ranch-style homes, the cul-de-sacs and winding streets lined by locust and maple trees prominent, and nary a hemlock to be found—all cut down at groundbreaking. Another irony. It was a neighborhood that Bob thought fit Peter perfectly: understated but solidly formed.

Peter had been a top-notch architect. Bob had toured some of his projects before and after, such as a rehabilitated mansion and a decrepit brick warehouse. All had been brought back to life, combining past and present into something efficiently beautiful.

When they had first moved in, Peter told Bob that he thought it only a couple of years before they would move on, purchasing a vacant property or a teardown. Peter would design a grand home with a basement, no less, which was not standard in Portland.

"But this house just seems right for us, Bob," Peter told him one evening after Beer & Horseshoes—a weekly warm-weather tradition at Bob's house with neighborhood guys—just the two of them sitting in Adirondacks, cold beer in hand. He looked around Bob's backyard, the sun setting into a purple-streaked sky. "Much like this beautiful old Victorian you live in seems to fit you like a well-worn glove, our house seems to fit me and Debra."

Bob parked in front of Peter's detached garage, which he had used as a workshop. Bob could picture pulling in on a Saturday morning, Peter manning the table saw, wearing his black Nikes, running shorts, and insignia-free gray T-shirt, in a cloud of sawdust as he cut a two-by-four or a sheet of plywood for one of his many projects.

Bob would give the horn a short toot and lean his head out the window. "Woodworking or cycling, Mr. Architect?"

Peter would look up, turn off the saw, and squint a smile at Bob. "Dr. Goodman, I presume?"

It became a routine that neither ever tired of: corny humor before a long bike ride, followed by a couple of beers and lunch at a local tavern.

Bob's gaze drifted over to the window box under the bay window of the family room, teeming with snapdragons, and then to his left, where Debra had kept up one of Peter's favorite projects— maintaining the yard with the laurel and azalea bushes along the picket fence and the lilac bush in the front, its mulch bed circled in a stone border. It seemed her way of honoring her husband.

Bob walked up the flagstone walk, which Peter had mortared over the existing concrete the first year they moved in. After completing the masonry job on the walk and front stoop, he had snipped shoots of English ivy from the brick wall at the entrance to Hemlock Hills, transplanting it along his front walk. "My first act of vandalism," he told Bob. "It is all the fault of that incorrigibly indestructible weed."

Devon greeted Bob silently at the front door with a look that said, *Let's hope for the best.*

The foyer flowed down two steps into the kitchen, where the granite countertops, stainless steel appliances, and glass-and-wood cabinets maintained a timeless quality. Debra was already seated at the table in the kitchen nook. The table was circular and large enough to seat six.

"Hello, Debra," Bob said as though he hadn't a care in the world.

Debra forced a smile. "Bob," she said with hesitancy.

"Have a seat, Dr. Goodman," Devon said.

Bob pulled back a chair and said, "Devon, how about you call me Bob from here on out. We're going to be partners for the next couple of weeks. Let's do away with the formalities."

"Sure," Devon said. "Bob it is."

Debra had a list of questions from which she began to read from: Where would they sleep? Would there be wild animals to contend with? What would they eat? What would happen if someone got injured? She looked up at Bob, her expression vague and unsettled, as though her mind was elsewhere. "I have more," she said in a hurried voice.

Bob said in a reassuring tone, "Our guide will fill us in on sleeping arrangements when we get there."

He offered a smile to Debra, whose expression remained tense as though a cord had been pulled tight from head to toe. "The terrain and weather is more a concern than the wildlife—"

Devon cut in. "Mom, we have to do this." He looked at Dr. Goodman for confirmation and then said to his mother, "I can't begin the rest of my life until I know Dad's status."

Debra glanced at her list and then looked at Devon, her eyes softening a bit, as she seemed to recognize that she too would like to know. "I do understand that," she said with a slight uptick of encouragement in her voice.

"Devon and I will not take any undue risks," Bob said. "I have spoken with our guide, Rudy Arredondo, and my impression is that he is a skilled, experienced man who will keep us safe. Plus, he speaks Quechua fluently. The trip shouldn't take more than two weeks."

Debra folded the list in half and then in quarters. "I am glad you are going with Devon, Bob," she said, smiling in such a way that her mouth didn't move and it was all in her fretful eyes. She moved the folded list off to the side. "What does Carey think of this?"

"She's upset that I'm not taking her with us."

Debra reached for Devon's hand and grasped it firmly. "Bob," she said with a sigh of resignation, "look after my boy. He's all I have left."

CHAPTER

4

After takeoff from Portland International Airport, Devon and Bob discussed their schedule in Peru. From Dr. Judd's documents, it seemed at least a three-day hike up the mountain to the village, if there really was a village. Devon sure hoped there was such a place, or this entire journey was for naught.

"I talked with our guide, Rudy," Bob said as he glanced out the window. Devon was in the middle seat, and the aisle seat was empty. "We have a meeting scheduled tomorrow at his office. Says he has wanted to return to find out what happened to your father ever since he found the body of Aldo Coreas. They were not just good friends but best friends. He feels an obligation for Aldo's sake."

"Did he mention anything about the climb?" Devon said as he leaned into Bob's space, pointing to the rising sun casting a golden splay of light over a sea of cumulus clouds.

"Beautiful," Bob said as he turned his attention away from the window. "He asked if we had been training for the trek up the mountain."

Both men had been exercising specifically for the climb ever since they decided to go. Devon did long runs carrying a full backpack crammed with gear. Bob had done cardio at his gym and long, hilly hikes. Devon thought him amazing for a man his age. Dr. Robert Goodman was a tall man with a fit, angular build from many years of a variety of physical activities, including mountain hiking.

Like his father, Devon had begun running when he joined the cross-country team in high school. At twenty-two, Devon was a lanky six foot three—nearly as tall as Bob Goodman—and his long legs were a big asset in gobbling up terrain. His father was shorter and more sturdily built: five foot ten and a half with thick, powerful legs. Devon never got the chance to run with his dad.

But what Devon really regretted was never having the opportunity to apologize to his father for the way he acted before his dad left for Peru. It was during a difficult social adjustment in his freshman year of high school; middle school friends had abandoned his friendship, throwing Devon into a funk.

Their last evening together, the waxing gibbous moon was occulting the northern section of the Pleiades. The naked eye star Maia would vanish behind the lunar disk, followed by the others before remerging on the other side of the moon, one after another.

Peter even had a quote from Tennyson hanging on his home office wall: "Many a night I saw the Pleiads, rising thro' the mellow shade, Glitter like a swarm of fire-flies tangled in a silver braid."

But Devon, out of sorts and upset with his father for deserting his family, told him that he was no longer interested in stargazing, leaving Peter to stargaze the Pleiades on his own.

Peter Richards had introduced his son to astronomy. They spent many an evening on the observation platform in the backyard, especially in the summer when there was no homework. His dad, who could build anything with his hands, had built the observation deck with retractable steps under the platform, which stood ten feet above ground and had post-and-timber railings. It was beautiful.

The telescope was an Orion Refractor. Sometimes during dinner, to give his father a hint, Devon would sneak peeks from the kitchen table in the direction of the closet where the telescope was stored and then glance at his father.

"Hey, Dev," his father would say with a wink, "what say after homework, we get out the tripod and Orion?"

But what was even better than stargazing in the backyard was camping out with his father, something young Devon looked forward to. He enjoyed packing up the car with the tent, pole, and stakes—by age ten, Devon could set up a tent by himself—cooking utensils, sleeping bag, and of course binoculars—Celestron Sky Master for father and son. Devon's first binoculars were small and much less powerful than his dad's huge, long lens pair, but for his thirteenth birthday, Devon had received a pair just like his father's.

After setting up camp and eating by campfire, they would break out their binoculars and find an open area to view the night sky. First up, they would find the moon and look for detail of its mountains and valleys, then maybe the Galilean moons of Jupiter, and always the Pleiades. Those sparkling blue gems, high in the eastern sky with a cascade of stars trailing down from the Dipper, shined so brightly on a clear night.

Peter's grandfather on his mother's side had introduced young Peter to stargazing, and he in turned passed it on to his son. So, for Devon to tell his father on the day before he was leaving for Peru, and possibly never returning home alive, that he no longer had any interest in stargazing had been a selfish act. For eight years, Devon had wished he could go back and stargaze one last time with his father.

◉

After arriving in LA, Devon and Bob had a long layover before boarding their flight for Peru. It was late afternoon, and the plane was only half-full. Bob told Devon to take the window seat, and he took the aisle.

It came over Devon how fortunate he was to have Bob along with him. His dad had been right—Bob Goodman was the smartest man in the room. Not only smart but organized and competent. He had set up the hotel reservation, contacted Rudy Arredondo, and studied all of the documents that Dr. Judd had turned over, including shaman testimonials, which Devon now had on his lap.

"There are some amazing stories in there, Devon."

"Really," Devon said as he scrolled through the three-ring notebook with articles and research papers in cellophane sleeves.

"There's one about an Indian native who made his living as a mountain guide until he injured his back in a fall. He was bedridden for nearly a year, then recovered enough to walk with a limp, but he was in constant pain. His back was out of place, and his hips were displaced. He was miserable.

"A friend knew of a shaman from his old village and arranged for the shaman to come to the guide's house. The shaman had the guide lie on the floor, and he sucked on the injured area and sang healing songs for three days."

"Three days?" Devon said, with a tone of incredulity.

"It was all documented," Bob said as he reached over, turned some pages, and tapped his finger on the pertinent article. "Then he was taken to the river, and the shaman bounced three kernels of corn, one by one, off his lower spine. The shaman then planted each kernel in a straight line, facing the sun, and said that when the stalks of corn grew, his back would be healed. For several years now, the guide has had no problems with his back and is back at work."

"I'd like to believe that, Bob," Devon said, "but ... his back could have healed on its own."

"That's true, Devon, but I like to think Shakespeare was on to something in regard to heaven and earth."

CHAPTER

5

By the time the plane touched down at Aeropuerto Internacional Jorge Chávez in Lima, it was midmorning. Devon had not slept a wink; his body was revved, similar to when he stayed up all night studying for finals. Bob, on the other hand, had dozed off into a comfortable sleep for the last four hours of the flight.

After Devon called his mother and Bob his wife to let them know they had landed, they took a cab to the hotel. The road was not a freeway but a large divided avenue. Up a ways, they turned off on to a long street lined with colonial Spanish-style buildings painted light pink and pale blue. Farther up, they came to a wider road that led to an open green circled by palm trees, and in its middle was a statue of a horseman atop a massive ornate base. A few blocks up, the taxi pulled into the circular drive of the hotel. "Same one my father stayed at," Devon said as the driver removed their gear from the trunk.

Bob said to the driver, "Uno momento, senor." He lifted a finger to indicate, *Just a moment.* "Regresaremos."

After leaving their gear at the front desk, Devon asked Bob on the way back to the cab, "Do you speak Spanish?"

"Enough to get me in trouble."

Inside the cab, Bob handed a note to the driver. "Nuestro destino."

The driver scanned it, looked into the rearview mirror, and nodded his approval. "Bueno, senor."

The taxi retraced its path past the open green and then turned down a couple of side roads before coming out on a freeway, with the Pacific Ocean on their left. After a couple of miles, the taxi exited the highway on to a two-lane road and turned left into the front of a cluster of condominiums rising high into the sky, an island of glass and steel.

After taking an elevator to the sixth floor, down the hallway they went to unit 604. From inside, Devon and Bob heard the melodic sound of a woodwind instrument. They exchanged looks before Bob knocked on the door.

Rudy Arredondo was youthful looking, with a robust, handsome face, radiant bronze skin, a strong, aquiline nose, and dark, alert eyes like a soldier on patrol. He held a rather primitive-looking wooden flute with six finger holes and a notched mouthpiece.

"Hello," Rudy said through an emerging grin, revealing a row of straight white teeth, similar to his aunt Vilma.

After Bob introduced himself and Devon and they shook hands, Bob said, motioning to the flute, "Is that a quena?"

"Yes," Rudy said with a look of surprise on his face.

"I have been studying Quechua culture."

"Ah," Rudy said with a concurring nod. He waved them inside. "Please come in."

They entered a large, spacious room. To their right was a wide hallway. A hardwood floor ran the length of the space. Along the way were a couple of hand-knotted throw rugs—one with a gray-and-white zigzag pattern, the other a geometric floral pattern. In the center of the room was a pair of leather armchairs with teak end tables, facing a matching three-cushion sofa, between them a ship's table with metal trim. Toward the front of the room and to their right was a granite countertop bar with four stools, which separated the kitchen. But what caught Devon's eye, which he stopped to get a better look at, was a mural on the wall of a row of snowcapped mountains overlooking a lush green valley. Soaring over the valley was a large-winged bird, its long feathers splayed out at the tips and a ruff of white feathers around the base of the neck.

"It looks like a large vulture," Devon said.

"El condor," Rudy said. "The Andean bird of myth." He pointed to a wide balcony with a view of the Pacific. "Let us sit and discuss our trek."

They sat at a round glass table with curved, wooden-slatted chairs with thick cushions. Below them was a spectacular view. To their right was a cliff that dropped down to the freeway, across which was a narrow beach and the sea-green Pacific. Devon wondered how Rudy could enjoy such plush accommodations on a guide's income.

After a brief chat about the flight over, they got down to business. "Tomorrow," Rudy said, "we shall drive north past Trujillo and will spend the night at a posada. Nine, maybe ten hours. Next day, we drive east to the mountains, where we stay below for a while."

"Stay below?" Bob said.

"The base of the mountain is higher than Lima, but where we go is very high. We must get some altitude in your blood before we climb the mountain."

Rudy glanced out at the ocean, then turned to face Devon. "Did you know," he said, "that I was a good friend of your father's guide, Aldo Coreas?"

Devon nodded as if to say, *Go on.*

"We discussed the journey before he departed. We will be following ..." He squinted as though searching for the right word.

"Footsteps?" Devon said.

"Their tracks to the mountain base, including staying at the rural posada en route—same as I took with the search party." Rudy folded his hands on the table as though for emphasis. "Soon it will be winter. We must go while the weather is still good." Rudy slid a look over at Bob. "High altitude and cold weather can cause problems for—"

Bob cut in. "For elderly folks like me." He lifted his brow toward Rudy. "I've climbed a few mountains in my day. I am looking forward to the challenge."

By the time Devon and Bob checked into their room, it was late afternoon. Devon was running on fumes. "Bob, I think I need a nap," he said, eyeing one of the two queen beds.

"Sure thing," Bob said, motioning with his eyes toward the window. "That's the Plaza de Armas."

Below them was a stretch of well-manicured greens and stonework the width of four street blocks, with a bronze fountain in the middle. Being the son of an architect and an engineering major, Devon had acquired an interest in buildings and how cities were designed. On the cab ride over, he had noted the old-style Spanish influence in the colonial-style structures with mauve walls and curved accolade windows in ornate, black iron frames.

Bob pointed to a twin-towered cathedral. "I wonder if your dad had time to tour the downtown."

"He did," Devon said. "He called my mother and me the evening he arrived and told us about walking about the city—took a horse-drawn carriage ride. He was duly impressed."

After Bob left for a walk about town, Devon punched his home number in his cell phone. "Hi, Mom."

"Devon," Debra said with a trace of trepidation in her voice.

Devon went over the meeting with Rudy. "We are going to follow the same route that Dad took to the mountain."

There was silence for a moment before Debra said, "Devon?"

"Yes, Mom."

"Please be safe. Please."

CHAPTER

6

At dawn in the hotel's circular drive, Devon and Bob crammed their backpacks in the back of Rudy's heavy-duty SUV, along with two five-gallon cans of gasoline, a box of dry goods, hiking boots, a nylon backpack stuffed with clothes, an assortment of miscellaneous camping gear, and a box sealed with duct tape.

Devon told Bob to sit in the front, and off they went. They drove around the Plaza de Araya, through the narrow streets lined with colonial-style buildings, and on to the divided avenue. Past the city limits, box houses popped up on a hillside.

Devon asked Rudy if those were where the poor people lived.

"Certainly not rich, but farther out from the city, the poverty is worse."

They turned on to a highway, with the Pacific Ocean on their left and nothing but open space and mountains ahead. Rudy said, "Nine, ten hours to posada."

Two hours into the trip, they drove along a desertlike coastline. Rudy lifted his chin. "There, the Andes."

Up ahead, a pale-blue outline of mountains loomed over the horizon.

"That is *magnifico*," Bob said.

Bob asked Rudy how he became a guide.

"Ah," Rudy said, "it is all the fault of Aldo Coreas." It turned out that Rudy's father worked at the Peruvian embassy in Washington, DC, for four years while Rudy was in grade school. "When we returned, my father was a liaison officer at the American embassy in Lima, and I became friends with an American boy whose house Aldo's mother cleaned."

Rudy lifted a finger as the sun was peeking over the mountains to their right, painting the sky and mountains in its golden light. "It is something, no?"

"Breathtaking," Bob said.

"Aldo used to come with his mother to clean, and the rest, as they say in your country, is history. We became inseparable, and after I finished college, my father wanted me to join the Foreign Service." Rudy paused and flickered a smile. "Aldo, who was already a mountain guide, took me camping for three days into the Andes."

Rudy took his hands off the wheel for a second and made an expression as if to say, *From then on, it was out of my hands.*

They turned off the highway into a desolate village. There was an adobe building with a gasoline pump in the front. Next to the front door was a wooden placard with *Comida* scrawled in bright red.

Rudy parked at the gasoline pump and went inside. He came back out with an old, barefoot woman in a flannel shirt and raggedy jeans. This was real poverty staring them in the face. Her gray hair was drawn back into a ponytail, and her deeply wrinkled face had a worn and tuckered-out look.

She said something to Rudy in Spanish, and he lifted the gas pump off its receiver and began filling the car. The old woman squinted hard for a moment at Bob and Devon, standing outside the car. In her small, dark eyes was a question. *Something out of the ordinary brings you here, no?* Then she made her way back inside the store.

Devon had the most overwhelming sense that his father had stopped here. It was as though he could feel a residue of his presence lingering in the cool, dry air. He looked up the rutted dirt street where there was a smattering of disheveled shed-like living quarters.

There was an emptiness about this little nothing place littered with five-gallon buckets and rusted shells of compact cars. Even with the scalloped russet hills rising up to meet a crystal-blue sky, this place could not be called anything but defeated. These people were far from the city in this mountainous land, but it came upon Devon that they did not live in the mountains—they existed. If his father had stopped here, he would have seen it the same way.

The old woman came back out of the store with a tray of three bowls of some sort of stew and a stack of flatbread. She placed it on a wooden table with four rickety-looking rattan chairs. Rudy paid her and said, "Gracias, senora." The old woman stole a glance at Devon, then went back inside.

The warm and spicy stew contained bits of potatoes, corn, and some colorful root vegetables. Devon was surprised that Bob didn't ask Rudy about the meal. But they were in a transitional state—not at their destination yet no longer in civilization. There had been a silent understanding that conversation should be kept to a minimum. They were now far away from whence they came. There were no safety nets out here.

CHAPTER

7

The adobe posada was situated on the side of a hill, overlooking the ocean, now shimmering in the afternoon light. The one-story, rectangular building, with rounded corners, was a faded eggshell color and appeared sturdy if roughly built, with a coarse finish on the walls. There was a serenity to this ordinary-looking posada backdropped by gnarly trees.

While Rudy checked in, Devon and Bob stood at the top of a set of timber-and-earthen steps carved into a scrubby hillside that went down to the shoreline.

When Rudy came up to them, he said, "The proprietor remembers your father, Devon."

"Really?"

"Yes, first gringo. You two are second and third."

"I sense," Bob said as he looked off to his right, a stone jetty the only trace of humankind's influence, "that will not be our last designation as second and third gringo."

"Let us clean up and meet over there for our meal," Rudy said as he pointed to a clearing of hard-packed earth on the side of the posada.

Devon's room had no door and was minimal, with a single bed, a washstand with basin, and a picture of Jesus on the wall. A communal toilet was at the end of the hall. Rudy had told him that he was staying in the same room as his father. Again, he felt his dad's presence, a lingering wisp of awareness before it vanished. This awareness was similar to what he had experienced when stargazing but stronger, like a Geiger counter getting closer to the source.

After washing up and a brief rest in the stiff-as-a-board bed, Devon joined Rudy and Bob outside.

Rudy said, "I will go to the sea and fish for our dinner," as he focused his gaze toward the ocean. "Devon and Roberto," he said, pronouncing their names with an emphasis on the second syllable—De-*vonn*, Row-*bur*-toe. He handed each a burlap sack. "If you could collect stones on the hillside this size for the firepit," he said, spreading his fingers apart, tips nearly touching. "And then if you could gather brush and downed tree limbs up there." He looked at a patch of scrub trees. "Two bagfuls, *por favor.*"

"Let's get the stones first," Bob said to Devon.

At the top of the hillside, Devon scanned the rocky incline—not too steep. He and Bob sidestepped their way down the slope, carefully avoiding the needles of spiny scrub plants and boulders wedged into the sandy soil, to collect stones the size of a fist.

Devon and Bob slung a quarter-full sack apiece of stones over their shoulders, steadied themselves, and climbed three steps and then a landing, three steps and then a landing, making their way up the hill.

The patch of gnarly, twisted trees reminded Devon of mesquite, and he wondered if, when his father stayed here, he had done the same chore and collected stones. The trees bore spines with yellow flowers and long greenish-yellow pods resembling peas.

Bob opened a pod to discover small brown seeds. He placed the tip of his tongue on a seed. "Surprisingly sweet," he said. "Sort of like wild honey."

Tufts of parched, long grass, twigs, and branches covered the ground. The grass came up with little resistance. They stuffed it in the sack along with the branches.

After Devon dug out the firepit with a camper's shovel, he placed the stones around it. "Just like with my dad when we camped out," Devon said as he spotted Rudy coming up the steps.

"We eat good dinner, amigos—*platijas*," Rudy hollered from the top step. He had a fishing rod in one hand and a string of flat fish in the other.

"Bravo, Rudy," Bob said with a big smile. "Bravo."

Devon reached for the string of fish, which looked similar to ocean flounder that he and his dad had caught at Depoe Bay off the Pacific Ocean on a fishing/stargazing weekend campout. "I'll clean them?" he said.

"Certainly," Rudy said.

While Devon cleaned the fish on a flat stone, Rudy and Bob emptied the bags of wood. "Ah, good," Rudy said as he balled up a clump of dead grass. "The huarango tree keeps all the earth's moisture. Greedy tree."

Rudy put the clump of grass in the pit, made a teepee of the smaller branches, and then stacked bigger branches around them.

After the fire died down to embers, Rudy began skewering the fish. "Good job, Devon." He lifted a finger and said, "Let me guess. Your father taught you how to clean fish."

"Yes," Devon said, nodding, "and many other things too that only now am I beginning to appreciate."

Peter Richards had shown his son how to savor the little things in life, like watching a striking sunset on a campout, its golden light sinking below the scarlet horizon. "Each sunset is a unique experience, Dev, choreographed by a star 93,000 million miles away."

When Devon was ten, he was helping his dad plant seeds in the raised garden bed in the backyard. Devon asked Peter if he had built the bed.

Peter was sitting on the edge of the cedar-planked bed, making small indents in the soil for seeds. "Yes, the year you were born. I did it with the help of a book written in the seventeenth century." Peter leaned forward. "See these?" he said as he ran his finger on a row of pegs connecting a corner. "Not a nail was used in the construction of this garden. All slots and pegs."

"Why?" Devon asked.

"Sometimes the old way is the better way. Nails can damage the wood."

Devon nodded and said, "Do you use the old way in your job?"

"I use the best of the old and new," Peter said as he reached into a plastic bag of kale seeds and began filling a row of half-inch holes. "Like salvaging old bricks on a jobsite but using modern methods of architecture."

"You like to build things, don't you, Dad?" Devon was standing across the bed from his father, tamping soil over the kale seeds.

"I like everything about the process." Peter looked over at his son, his eyes seeking Devon's.

In his father's gaze, Devon saw for the first time the depth of his father.

❈

At dawn, they departed the posada. After a while, they saw hardly a car or truck.

"Soon we will gain altitude," Rudy said as they passed a cluster of adobe structures at the end of a dirt road off the highway. He said they were on the central highway that ran the length of Peru. "Panamericana Norte, numero uno."

The green-blue ocean below stretched out to the pale horizon. To their right, behind the village, ocher-colored hills slanted upward until land met sky.

An hour past the rural village, other than the road, there was no trace of civilization. Ahead, the snowcapped Andes dominated the landscape like giant sentries.

They turned off the highway, rattling along a valley floor, the mountains closing in on them.

Farther up, Rudy slowed down as they banged and bumped along over the rocky, rutted ground. They drove parallel to a stream speckled with boulders and with stones bordering its shoreline. Past it was a series of foothills. Nearby was a field of wild grass, and past that was a stretch of undulating terrain, ending at the base of a mountain shrouded in mist.

"What a sight," Bob said. "What a mountain."

"And so it begins," Devon said.

"Look over there." Rudy pointed to an adobe hut with a thatched roof and a hide flap doorway. "It appears that *providencia* is with us," he said as he brought the car to a stop.

They got out of the car, and Rudy led them into the hut. The dirt floor was empty.

"When I came with the search party, someone was living here, maybe a shepherd, though we never saw him or anyone during the entire search up to the bridge," Rudy said with a shrug. "Come. Let us gather our gear."

After setting up their sleeping bags, they went outside. While Rudy dug a shallow pit, Bob and Devon went down to the stream with a gunny sack. Rudy had told them to collect enough stones for a firepit, plus one flat one.

After the fire had settled down, Rudy placed the flat stone over the red-hot embers. He emptied a generous portion of potatoes on a cloth and then loaded the spuds on metal skewers. He laid the skewers on top of the flat stone, turning them every so often. They sat in silence, waiting for the potatoes to cook.

When the potatoes were done, Rudy handed tin plates to Devon and Bob. Then from his backpack, he took out a roll of stringy dried beef from a plastic bag. He peeled off a portion and handed it to Bob and then one to Devon.

During the meal, Rudy said, "I have brought enough potatoes and firewood to last us for the three days at the mountain base. After that, it will be beef jerky, flatbread, and quinoa." He carefully pulled a potato from his spit and blew on it. "We must travel as light as possible," he said, lifting his chin toward the mountain, now a dark outline in the fading light, "to climb that monster."

"What is the schedule for the days here below?" Bob said as he removed the cap from his canteen and took a swig.

"We will walk those *estribaciones*," Rudy said, pointing toward the foothills over by the stream."

"Sort of like boot camp," Devon said as he rolled a hot potato in his fingers.

"Yes," Rudy said as he stole a glance at the mountain looming over them. "We must get conditioned to carry the weight of the pack and get our lungs prepared for the challenges that lie ahead."

CHAPTER

8

As the sun rose over the mountains to the east, they began the training exercise, carrying full backpacks. They walked in silence, Rudy leading, occasionally looking back, waiting, and then pushing on as they maneuvered their way up and down, around and over ridges, fissures in the land, steeps, and inclined screes littered with loose rock. Bob's main concern was not to catch his foot in the crevices of the uneven terrain.

By the time they stopped to eat, Bob was winded. They ate flatbread and meat strips on the side of a foothill. "This reminds me of the forced march we took in OCS," Bob said.

"You were in the army?" Devon asked.

"No," Bob said with a shake of his head. "I was in the navy. They paid for med school, so I owed them four years of duty."

"Did you go to sea?" Rudy said as he studied Bob for a moment as though seeing him in a new light.

"The year was 1968, and America's combat involvement in Vietnam was ratcheting up, and doctors were needed. I was assigned to the Sixty-Fourth Medical Group at the evacuation hospital in Da Nang." Bob looked off as though seeing long ago. "I will never forget flying in, between China Beach and Monkey Mountain.

"Da Nang is a port city on the Eastern Sea—Shangri-la come to life with the lush green hills, crystal-blue water, and white-sand beaches." He took a bite of his beef jerky and washed it down with a swig of water from his canteen. "I never thought I would see anything so hauntingly beautiful." He pointed to a string of snowcapped mountains in the distance. "Until I came here. Two different environments, but both had the same effect on me at first sight."

After eating, Rudy continued to push them over the foothills that were low slung at the base but quickly rose into steep, choppy slopes of rust-colored, hard earth. Behind the foothills were larger hills splintered into a diversity of hues from shadow to sunlight.

Bob was taking it all in with his *forward* mantra. Breathing in the stingy, arid air, he and Devon pushed themselves to keep up with Rudy, who was a walking machine that never seemed to tire.

This land seemed a forgotten place, untouched by civilization, which had endured through the ages, a place of unconquerable spirit that had escaped the grip of humankind. Bob had been to many lands, mostly across Europe, Asia, and Africa, but this place had a uniqueness in not only the rugged terrain but something else—an aura of beyond the here and now.

Bob saw in Devon's eyes that he too had been captured by this faraway land. The young man walked with enthusiastic vigor, not saying much but seeming to absorb his surroundings as though preparing himself for what lay ahead.

And what exactly did lay ahead? Rudy had a copy of the map to the collapsed bridge, drawn by a member of his search team who found the body of Aldo Coreas. But that route could only take them so far—to a fork in the trail where they would have to take another way. From there, Rudy said he would use his navigational skills to get them up the mountain.

Rudy was confident that he could figure an alternative route up the mountain. "If Olaquecha does exist—and I believe it does," Rudy had told his companions last night before turning in, "then there will be other trails to the top besides the swinging bridge of the vines of the maguey plant that took my friend's life."

If Peter had witnessed his guide's death going up the mountain, then the cancer would have spread, and Peter would most certainly have been dead for years, but wouldn't the search team have found his remains?

And if Peter and Aldo had made it to the shaman and Peter had miraculously been cured, then there was a chance that he had somehow made it back to the village after Aldo's death at the bridge. Peter's survival for all this time was a long shot for sure but one Bob thought worth considering, especially with a competent guide like Rudy, who could discuss the composition of the earth and minerals they were walking over. "This red soil is made of rock fragments and is called *latosoles* and contains iron and tin," he said in passing.

Bob realized that this undertaking had an element of danger to it—more than he had experienced since his tour of duty in Vietnam. The first couple of months, Bob operated on infantrymen brought in from the field with shrapnel and frag wounds. It was a shock to see the excess blood and soldiers and marines missing limbs. One soldier had lost all four of his limbs and was still conscious; he would never forget the horror on the young man's face. It was gruesome work, but it was excellent training, and the hospital was well staffed with thirty doctors and sixty nurses.

Then one night, in the middle of Bob's tour, he was awakened from his bunk by a powerful series of *kabooms* off in the distance. The NVA had launched fifty 122-mm rockets in the span of one minute on the airbase. He raced to the Quonset hut window to see the sky ablaze in a crimson-and-yellow blanket of fire.

Soon after, the phone rang, and Bob and his bunkmates—all medical personnel—were ordered to the hospital to assist with mass casualties. Bob dressed quickly, threw on his flak jacket and helmet, and raced to the hospital across the street. Later, he learned that the damage at the airbase was extensive: eight men dead and 173 wounded, plus ten aircraft, one barracks, and a bomb dump destroyed. Forty other aircraft were damaged.

Wounded men, some with limbs missing, others battered and bloody from the attack, were filling the OR. Under the guidance of his commanding doctor, Bob helped get the wounded stitched up, giving IVs and whatever was needed. He was in surgery for twenty-four hours straight. At the end of it, Bob stumbled back to his barracks a changed man.

Once out of the military, Lieutenant Robert Goodman promised himself that he would live this life for all it was worth. He would travel to medical conferences all over the world to experience the cultures, to soak it all in, and to always look forward. Always.

For three days, they walked the foothills, each day Rudy pushing them farther. And each day, Bob and Devon gained endurance, their recent training and years of physical exertion paying off, though both were sore in their thighs and shoulders. Bob had purchased new boots, which he had barely broken in back home, but they were light and durable. His feet were adjusting to them, resulting in blisters on his toes, a small inconvenience in comparison to trekking up Olaquecha Mountain.

After the third day of hiking, Rudy led Bob and Devon to the back of his SUV. "We must pack light for the journey mañana." He checked over both their backpacks and the content Bob had purchased for himself and Devon: two lightweight but thermal sweater shirts, four pairs of brief underwear and undershirts, two windbreakers, two pairs of hiking pants, and four pairs of lightweight wool hiking socks.

"I let you carry your heavy packs for training," Rudy said as he dug into the back of the cargo area and opened the box that been duct taped. "I have lighter, better packs that will make the journey easier." Aldo pulled out a pair of sleek-looking nylon backpacks and handed one to each man.

"That is nice," Bob said as he looked at Devon, who had slipped his on his back. "I hardly feel it," Devon said.

Rudy then removed from the box two nylon bedrolls and handed one to each man.

"Will it keep us warm?" Devon asked as he unzipped the roll and ran his hand inside a tightly stitched fleece liner.

"Yes," Rudy said, "it will keep you warm but it weighs less than half a kilo." He lifted his brow to Bob. "What do you think, Roberto?"

"I think," Bob said through an emerging smile, "that Devon and I are in good hands."

CHAPTER

9

After eating, the three men retired to the hut and their sleeping bags. During the meal, Rudy had noticed a turning inward as the moment of truth was upon them. He liked that his traveling companions were quiet men who seemed to realize the gravitas of what they were to about to embark on.

Rudy shifted on to his side, his back against the rear wall, Devon and Bob lying across the space from each other. Bob was already sound asleep, his breathing slow and even. Devon, though, Rudy sensed was still awake. *It must be an unimaginable feeling to have lost one's father eight years ago and not have resolution. This trek,* Rudy thought as he turned on his back, fingers laced behind the nape of his neck, *will be a challenge.*

Bob's age could come into play at some point. The good doctor had spirit and was in fine condition, but the strenuousness and exertion required to climb the mountain, and in that altitude, had a way of sapping the will of older climbers. Rudy had seen this occur over the years with men and women in their fifties and sixties who thought they were invincible. They would curl up in the fetal position, wheezing for air.

If any member of their three-man party had such an attack, it would throw the entire project into question. The victim would have to be taken down to a lower altitude, and then what? Allow him to recover and then go back up again, waiting for a repeat to occur?

Rudy had also seen mountain sickness strike the young—and without warning. One moment a person was fine, and within minutes, the chest tightened, there was coughing, fluid filled the lungs—a variety of sicknesses could befall them. But then there were the ones with no problems, and some of them were seniors. One man, in his seventies, climbed with Rudy step for step for three days, with nary a complaint or hesitation. Afterward, he did admit that his body was "one big sore." But on all those climbs, Rudy had a safety net, a backup plan in case of emergency. Here in this mountain wilderness, they were on their own—completely.

Unlike Bob, Devon had youth on his side, but with youth came inexperience. However, he had much outdoor experience with his father, and like Bob, he was in excellent physical condition. He seemed mature for his age; losing one's father as a teenager can make one grow up in a hurry.

During the last meal at the mountain base, Devon pointed to the dusky sky as the first sign of the Pleiades emerged in a flickering tail of silver. "Look. The Seven Sisters are inverted in the Southern Hemisphere. I knew that, but actually seeing them upside down is ..."

"A pleasant discovery," Bob said.

"Yes," Devon said. "My father has been fascinated by that group of stars since his boyhood."

Rudy first learned of this star cluster when he visited Aldo's grandfather Quayo's Quechua village. It was the first time Rudy came in contact with his roots on his mother's side. It had a profound effect on him, as did the Star Search their first night. At the edge of the village in a clearing, Quayo pointed up at the night sky. "Killa, Puka Qoullor." (Moon, Red Star, Mars.) He scrolled his finger up and over to his left. "Ah," Quayo said in a tone of reverence. "Collca." (Storehouse.) The Quechua people believed the brightness of the Pleiades indicated when to plant crops.

46

"The Pleiades," Bob had said as he stared into the hot embers of the fire, "are important to many agrarian cultures."

Rudy wondered if there wasn't a connection between Peter Richards's fascination with the Seven Sisters and his journey to find a Quechua shaman. And perhaps there was a greater purpose why they had been brought together.

They were three men, each from a different generation, each with a reason for wanting to climb Olaquecha. Devon's was the most important, wanting to discover the status of his father. Bob had mentioned to Rudy that Peter Richards's search for a shaman and a cure for his illness was at Bob's behest. Rudy wanted to bring closure to Aldo's last climb.

This climb to the top of the mountain was unlike any Rudy had ever done, ascending a mountain of myth far away from civilization. He had heard of Olaquecha and the Qusmi Runa (Cloud People), who legend had it lived in a remote village, high and hidden, far up the mountain.

He had learned this not from a Peruvian but the husband of his aunt Vilma, an American archaeologist, Dr. Neil Judd. Uncle Neil believed that it was not only possible that the village of Olaquecha existed "but more than likely." He had done extensive research on the subject and came to believe in its existence. "One of the last great mysteries still out of the reach of civilization," he had told Rudy.

Eight years ago, when Aldo had told Rudy that he was taking an Americano with a terminal illness in search of the village of Olaquecha and its shaman, Rudy thought it risky, not only for Peter Richards, who, with his sickness, was putting himself in grave danger trying to climb such a rugged mountain, but also Aldo. Uncle Neil had recounted tales of men losing their lives in search of Olaquecha, and from the moment Aldo had spoken of his plan, Rudy felt uneasy, as though there were powers at play that went beyond the scope of general knowledge.

At first light, they departed. By the time they reached the trailhead, the wind had died down and the gray sky had turned a silvery blue.

Rudy took off his backpack and removed the wooden flute he had played at his condo. "I am going to play a song on my quena to the mountain spirits for safe passage," he said. He looked at Devon and then Bob, a question in his eyes.

"Wonderful," Bob said. "Please, by all means, play your quena."

Rudy played for five minutes, starting out in a low reedy pace and then adding *micha* (oomph) toward the end.

When he finished, Bob said, "That was beautiful, almost like another wind blowing with an ethereal, penetrating quality."

"It is even better when played with a partner," Rudy said as he packed the flute and tugged his backpack up his shoulders. He made a sweeping gesture toward the mountain. "Especially in the land of sky and mountain, where the music is free to dance with the wind." He turned to his companions. "Are you ready, amigos?"

"I am," Bob declared in a strong, enthusiastic voice as he looked up at the mountaintop obscured by a bank of fleecy white clouds.

"Me too," Devon said. "Let us get up this great mountain."

The trail started out at a reasonable incline, but Rudy said soon enough it would get steeper in parts, as he checked over the map to the collapsed bridge, intricately drawn with a scale of one millimeter per kilometer, compass rose, and key telling what the symbols on the map represented.

This trail was like many Rudy had hiked over the years, bordered by rocky walls and boulders of all sizes, and was plenty wide enough for three men to walk side by side.

During the training hikes, Rudy had been pleased at how well both his companions had managed, but this mountain was another story. He had packed something in his woven pouch attached to his belt that would help all of them on their journey.

Farther on, they passed an expanse of grassland with an array of wildflowers struck with color. "How are you feeling, amigos?" Rudy said with a glance to his left and right.

"Fine," they both said in unison, a bit too quickly.

"Let us stop and rest for a moment," Rudy said.

They sat on a flat-topped boulder with a view of the colorful field of flowers.

All three opened their canteens and drank. "Amigos," Rudy said, "you must let me know if you are getting fatigued." He lifted a cautionary finger. "Especially if you begin to feel light-headed."

"I'm okay," Devon said as he screwed the cap back on his canteen.

"Roberto?"

"A little short of breath," Bob said, "but hopefully my body will adapt." He removed his stocking cap and ran his hand through his steel-gray hair. A thin smile creased the corner of his lip. "I have always been able to adapt to a new environment, Rudy. Let us hope," he said, spreading his hands out in front of him, "Olaquecha Mountain will not break my streak."

CHAPTER

10

round noon, they came to a terraced section of rocky
steps leading down to an obelisk of stones in a field of
wildflowers that overlooked the valley.

"Let us eat," Rudy said.

They sat on the steps, Rudy and Bob at the top, Devon down
a flight.

All three drank from their canteens.

Rudy handed each man a tin plate and then removed from his
pack four plastic bags. From one he removed three triangular-
shaped rolls, and from the other bags he emptied a portion of tiny
yellow grain pellets onto their plates.

"Raw quinoa?" Bob asked.

"Yes," Rudy said. "It's raw and crunchy, but there is much
protein in these tiny seeds. You must chew them thoroughly to
get the most benefit."

Devon took a small handful and chewed and chewed before
swallowing. "Bob, with a diet like this, we should have fattened
ourselves up before departure." He washed it down with a swig of
water.

All three began to eat in earnest and in silence, other than Rudy
looking over his companions and reminding them to let him know
if they needed to rest.

After they ate, Devon shielded his eyes from the sun, checking its position in the sky.

"Are you reading the time from the sun?" Rudy said.

Devon made a face to indicate, *Sort of.* "My father could tell the time from the sun's position within a minute."

Rudy stood. "He was—*is* a starman. Where we go, the people believe the stars have great power—regarding when to plant and harvest crops." He placed his foot on the top step and tied a loose shoelace. "Also," Rudy added, "the prophesying elders read the stars and predicted future events. In my ancestors' world, these beliefs were unchallenged."

"I have been to enough places on this great earth," Bob said as he stood and stretched his long arms over his head, "to believe there are things that science cannot explain." He slipped into his pack and lifted his chin to indicate, *One more thing.* "And at medical conferences, I have talked to physicians who have seen dying patients miraculously heal."

"I'd say, Dr. Goodman," Devon said as he stepped up onto the trail, "that it is time for you to witness your own medical miracle firsthand—us finding my father alive."

Rudy said, "I have something to help on our trek up the mountain." He handed both men dried green leaves the size of bay leaves from the pouch on his hip. "Do not chew but suck on these as you climb."

Devon spread the thin, oval leaves in his hand. They were opaque and tapered at the extremities yet gave the impression of hardiness.

"*Fruta de coca* for our journey." Rudy pinched a couple of leaves into a wad and stuffed it in the side of his mouth. He then removed what looked like a white rock from a plastic bag in his pack. He cut off a sliver with a pocketknife. "Do not put this lime near your lips but back with the coca leaves. Watch how I do it." He wedged the lime in with the coca leaf.

He handed Bob and Devon a sliver of lime. "This will help with the altitude and other things."

It did not take long for the coca to numb Devon's mouth and soon after lessen his fatigue. He was pretty tired at lunch but didn't want to say anything, especially since Bob seemed to be handling the trek well.

As they came to a level stretch of trail, Rudy said, "Do you feel the coca, amigos?"

"Bueno," Bob said.

"Good," Devon said.

"You two sound like Quechua Indians—men of few words." Rudy turned to Bob and said, "Aldo had a saying: in the silence of the mountain, there is much you can learn."

Over the course of the afternoon, they climbed at a steady pace, stopping twice for water breaks. Devon's breathing remained good, but he began tugging at the straps of his backpack as his shoulders grew tired from the weight. Bob was beginning to show signs of fatigue, his expression a grimace as he strove onward.

They took a breather, sitting on a rock bordering the trail.

"We must push on while the weather is good," Rudy said. "But we must know our limit."

Devon glanced at Rudy as he took a swig of water from his canteen. His guide was built similar to his father, Peter, with a strong, sturdy body anchored by square shoulders that tapered down to the waist. "What did your family say when you became a guide?"

"At first, disappointment, for sure, that I didn't go into the Foreign Service, but then my mother and father saw how happy I was. Money was not a factor in my family; my grandfather was a wealthy businessman, and at age thirty, I inherited a sizable amount of money."

Rudy ran his hand back and forth over the gritty surface of the rock. "I take people to the ancient ruins and explain the Andean culture—and more so the Quechua culture that I have been fascinated with for years." He looked off for a moment as though trying to find the right words. "Aldo was half-Quechua, and he took me to his grandfather's village." He stared off for a moment, a glint in his eyes. "The simplicity yet substance of their lives in that Quechua village never left me." He took a swig from his canteen and wiped his mouth with the back of his hand. "Here," he said, spreading his hand out to the side, "far from the city's influence, this mountain of legend is putting its grip on me."

CHAPTER

11

Late afternoon, they came to a promontory jutting out of the side of the mountain. On one side was a cliff dotted with stone huts on a ledge that spanned the width of the cliff, and in the middle of the promontory was a stretch of wall with recesses supported by columns and lintels, all linked together by massive stones.

On the near side of the cliff, narrow steps had been cut into the mountainside, leading up to the huts.

"Looks deserted," Devon said.

"Long, long time," Rudy said as he gestured toward the stone huts on the cliff, each with an arched entry and no windows. "Tonight, we will sleep under the cover of the mountain."

"Let's have a look around," Bob said.

After dropping their packs on a raised stone near the wall, Bob peeked into a recess that was large enough for an adult to stand in. "Is this what I think it is?" Bob said to Rudy.

"Human sacrifice chambers." Rudy arched his brow and nodded. "The shamans would pick out members of their tribe. Young women and children were sacrificed to the Pleiades to sustain the universe."

"Really?" Devon said.

"Yes," Rudy said. "Brutal they were in execution—stoning, mutilation, strangulation." Rudy looked at the sky as the sun slid behind a cloud, casting a shadow over the mountain. "So advanced in some ways and so backward in others."

"The history of mankind," Bob said as he turned his attention to Devon, trying to fit the tip of his pocketknife between the massive stones.

"Look at how tight this workmanship is," Devon said. For the third time on this journey, he had an overwhelming sense that his father had been here. If so, he would have been fascinated by how these enormous stones were put in place with such precision.

"If I remember it so, there should be wood for fire and water across the trail," Rudy said.

They headed back up the trail, crossing it and going past a shingly scree to a wide expanse of rocky terrain.

Past a mound of stones at the end of the rocky terrain, they came to a clearing of hard-packed earth with shrubby, gnarled trees growing in the earth and between fissures in the rock. Twisted and gnarled branches and limbs were scattered below the trees.

"Up ahead, water," Rudy said.

Past the clearing, they came to a pool of water surrounded by sharp crested ridges and finger-shaped stones. Water trickled down the face of a rocky cliff directly across from where they stood.

"Bueno," Rudy said. "We will fill our canteens. But don't drink the water until we get back to camp."

They returned to an open area on the promontory, with full canteens and armfuls of the down branches.

"I brought iodine tincture," Bob said as he removed an eye dropper from his backpack. "This mountain water may well be safe, but we don't want to take a chance."

"Hah," Rudy said. "I also brought it."

"Great minds think alike," Devon said as Bob dosed all three canteens.

As dusk fell over the land, they sat Indian style at the fire, eating raw quinoa and flatbread and beef jerky that Rudy had warmed on a flat stone.

Devon was tired, very tired. His neck and shoulders ached, his thighs were like spaghetti, and all he wanted to do was eat and go to sleep. Bob had a weariness about his countenance—the corner of his lips in a downward slant, the eyes a thin squint, and robotic movements as he ate. Devon couldn't tell if Rudy was tired or not. He wondered if it was part of a guide's code of conduct to never reveal fatigue.

Rudy took a bite of his jerky, followed by a chomp of his bread, swelling his cheek. "Tomorrow, we should come to where we take the trail away from the direction of the bridge." He took a swig of water from his canteen and looked at Bob. "Roberto, from here on out, we travel by our instincts up this great mountain. What do you think?"

"Lead the way, Rudy."

Devon woke in the middle of the night with a start. The darkness was so intense he was unable to see his hand in front of his face. His father had come to him in a dream, dressed in a poncho—the color of a rose in full bloom. His hair, no longer short and neat, was long and tied in a ponytail, and his face had a scraggly beard that belonged on a homeless man. His dad was speaking in a strange tongue—Quechua? But he understood what he was saying. "Stay away, Devon," Peter said with both hands extended. "It is not safe for you to come here." Devon's father gravely shook his head. "Please return to your mother. *Please.*"

For the remainder of the night, Devon could not get the fearful expression on his father's face out of his mind. His eyes were like glowing black beads screaming fear for his only child.

The morning light crept through the opening of the stone hut, accompanied by the faint tremor of a flute whispering in Devon's ear. Music and light, light and music—so subtle yet so appropriate to arrive in tandem.

Rudy must be playing. Out there in no-man's-land, the music took hold of Devon. How ethereal it sounded.

He sat up in his sleeping bag, feeling the tightness in his calves and thighs from yesterday's climb, his back stiff from sleeping on the hard surface. Today would be a challenge. Devon shimmied out of his bedroll as the chilled morning air greeted him. He undressed to his waist and washed his face and upper body with a handful of water from his canteen and a bar of soap. He pat-dried himself with a sock and then dressed.

On the cliff ledge, to Devon's surprise, he was greeted by Rudy, his flute at his side. He too had heard the music. Bob then emerged from his hut.

Rudy pointed down below to a man sitting cross-legged, playing a flute—an Indian wearing shin-length trousers, a gray poncho, and a rolled mat bundle strung across his shoulder blades. Atop his head was a knitted cap with a tasseled end. His face had a bronze hue, and his ruddy cheekbones were high and wide, sweeping down to a strong, prominent chin. A fire was burning, and there were irregular-shaped tubers—red and yellow—warming on a stone.

"Ah," Rudy said, "we are in luck. Let us go down and greet this mountain minstrel who plays the quena."

As they approached, the Indian continued to play, as though lost in his private world of reedy notes.

They sat in a circle, Rudy facing the Indian. Their tubular instruments were similar, each with six finger holes and openings at both ends. Rudy's was more refined, with polished wood and green and orange bands painted toward the bottom.

Their music rose from dry and hollow overtones to mellow wafting seemingly floating in air as their fingers danced along the finger holes. The sounds emitted from the two wooden instruments melded into a textured and dark timbre, as though emerging from the soul of this great mountain. It was as free as the wind, and the rhythm and power of the music seemed to stir Rudy, suggesting a passion for the rediscovered.

After a few minutes, the music stopped, and Rudy and the Indian seemed to awaken from their trancelike state.

Rudy said something to the Indian in Quechua, and the man responded in a slow, steady patois.

"Amigos, allow me to introduce you to Yachay."

CHAPTER

12

Yachay stood at the fire and lifted a steaming tuber overhead. "Dios pagarasunki."

Rudy said, "He is thanking the mountain for our meal."

Yachay pointed toward the tubers. "Mikui."

Devon had a thousand questions to ask Yachay, but he sensed that he must not rush—that it might be impolite to discuss his father until after the meal. He looked at Bob, who lifted his fingers slightly to indicate, *Wait.*

The tubers, which Rudy said were called *oca*, were a welcomed treat. Though not completely cooked, they tasted like lemony potatoes with a trace of nutty flavor.

Bob twirled a hot oca in his hand and took a hearty chomp. He shot a look at Rudy and said in a low voice, "After we eat, we powwow?"

Rudy nodded, his expression unchanged.

Bob and Devon exchanged looks. The moment of truth could well be upon them.

Devon thought there were three things that could happen: Yachay could know nothing about his father or the village of Olaquecha—doubtful. Yachay could inform them that his father was dead. Or he could say that he was alive. Only one of the three possibilities would send them back down the mountain.

Bob said to Rudy. "How do you say *thank you* in Quechua?"

"Agradiseyki," Rudy said in a low voice as he leaned toward Bob.

Bob raised his half-eaten tuber toward Yachay. "Agra dis i koo key."

The Indian tilted his head toward Bob. "Imamanta."

After they ate, Yachay, whose expression had remained a blank slate, looked around the circle of men, looking each in the eye. He said to Rudy, "Hamuy Padura?"

Rudy spoke in a composed yet forceful manner, a series of tongue twisters rolling out of his mouth. The only word Devon recognized was Olaquecha.

Now, Yachay spoke with animated vigor. His once placid face was alive, the dark eyes intense with concentration, and the voice strong but with an inflection of warning as he used his brown hands for emphasis.

Rudy and Yachay spoke for a few minutes that seemed to Devon an eternity. When they had finished talking, Rudy looked at Bob and then Devon. "Your father is alive."

Devon felt his jaw gape. He looked at Bob, trying to find the words.

"Is he sure?" Bob said.

Rudy said, "He rescued your father, Devon."

Devon felt a surge in his chest as though he had been electrified. He stared at Yachay to confirm what he had heard.

Yachay nodded and said, "Padura kawsay."

There was such a stripped-down honesty about this man, this Indian, Yachay, that Devon knew he was telling the truth. "My father is alive. Alive!"

Not only was Peter Richards alive, but what Yachay also had to say was astounding. Before Peter's arrival, the shaman, Attu, dreamt that the reincarnate of Padura, a great Quechua leader from long ago, would return home in need of assistance.

In a grand ceremony in front of the entire village, Peter Richards was cured by Attu with a combination of a potion and his healing touch.

After the ceremony, Peter was informed by Attu that he was the reincarnate of Padura and that he had returned home to his people.

The next day, the shaman took Peter to a secret location and showed him drawings on the wall of a cave to indicate that Padura was a starman from the Pleiades who was summoned to Earth by Viracocha, the creator. The shaman did not want Peter to leave the village and warned that there would be big trouble if he left.

Disregarding the shaman's warning, Aldo and Peter departed the village at first light. Three days later, Yachay found Devon's father near death on the side of the trail after spending the night in a blizzard. Yachay said, "Millagru." (Miracle.) He squinted and nodded at Devon. "Attu, hatun kallpa." (The shaman has big power.)

During his recovery at Yachay and his son's mountainside abode, Peter told Yachay that on their second day down the mountain, he had witnessed Aldo fall to his death when the bridge of maguey vines collapsed from a powerful gust of wind that appeared out of nowhere. Peter said it was the work of the shaman, and Yachay agreed.

When Peter was well enough, he made a walking sign with his fingers and said to Yachay, "Olaquecha … Attu." He wanted Yachay to guide him back to the village and the shaman. Yachay signaled he would guide him down the mountain, but Peter crossed his hands back and forth. "No, Yachay, no." He was adamant; he would not be responsible for another man's death.

Over time, Peter Richards assimilated into life in the village and became a revered figure by its people. He learned the rudiments of the Quechua language and joined in the planting and harvest and celebrations, where on each occasion the shaman would thank Viracocha for returning Padura, who brought good fortune to Olaquecha.

Yachay, who had left the village years before in a dispute with the shaman, snuck in from time to time to see his woman and son.

"Padura manchakuy lluqsly Olaquecha." (Padura remains afraid to leave Olaquecha.)

Yachay went on to say that he would guide them to the edge of the village, but they must not enter with the shaman present. "Nuqa rimay Padura." (I will speak with Padura.)

Bob said, "Peter could well be suffering from agoraphobia. Though he doesn't want to stay in the village, he most likely sees no way out."

Devon had so many questions about his father, but he held his tongue. The only important thing now was getting him out of the village and back down the mountain to safety.

CHAPTER

13

Rudy and Yachay led them up the mountain double file, all with a chaw of coca leaf and lime between cheek and gum. Before Peru, Bob had never taken this medicinal plant. He had read about its curative effects, and it did help relieve the soreness and provide a lift to his spirit.

Walking up this remote mountain and breathing the invigorating air had activated a sensory awareness in Bob. He sensed there were powers at work—conflicting powers—that had led Yachay to them. Would Rudy have been able to guide them to Olaquecha? Maybe, but at what cost to their limited supplies, their physical condition, which was already being tested, and their mental outlook? They were all critical to a successful mission.

Bob had heard many things in his world travels in regard to the supernatural, but the shaman healing Peter, claiming Peter was the reincarnate of a starman, and then the eerie death of Aldo Coreas and Peter's miraculous survival were by far the most compelling. Lives were at stake.

It had been eight years since Peter had been home, and with many patients in that situation, Bob would have worried about them adjusting to their previous lives, with the inevitable changes at home, work, and in the community that had developed over time: reacquainting oneself with a wife and child and all the dynamics of family life; getting one's mind around living on a schedule of work and social life; driving a car in traffic; and hearing the industrial sounds of civilization after the silence of the mountain. He worried about Peter returning to his architectural firm, getting back to speed on projects and new technology, and reconnecting with his partners and employees. All of it could be overwhelming, but Peter was a pragmatic, determined man, strong of body and mind, a good man who loved his family and his work with an undeniable passion. Yes, there would be some adjustments, but if they could convince Peter to leave, Bob felt confident that he would adjust quickly.

Bob squinted up the steep trail. Off in the pale-blue distance, a line of mountains with crests of glittering snow rose into the infinite sky. It seemed a timeless, vast place, so strange and so daunting and, dare he say it, so very alluring.

By noon, they were descending into a gorge with a smattering of snow in the shadows along the trail's border. A ways back, they had passed the fork in the road, which had one route, to their right, leading to the fallen bridge of maguey vines. Yachay pointed to the trail on his left, without any acknowledgment to the other trail.

Around a bend, up ahead, the trail was a long, steady decline. They were going around and down and, Bob imagined, then up to compensate for the downed bridge. He wondered if Peter and Aldo had sensed an inherent danger in crossing the bridge after the shaman's warning. Maybe Aldo had gone first because of such fear.

Rudy and Yachay came to a halt. Both looked over their shoulders, checking on Bob and Devon. "How are you doing, Roberto?"

"Hanging in there," Bob said. Every part of his body ached, from his sore feet, up his legs and arms, up his torso, and of course his neck and shoulders. But he didn't want to be any sort of distraction to the mission at hand.

Physical pain was not new to Bob. He had been on mountain hikes across the globe. But in those hikes, all he carried was a light waist pack, and each daily destination had a hot shower, clean clothes, good food, and a warm bed waiting.

Out here, they were on their own, with their survivalist food and clothes and bedrolls on their backs. There were no rescue parties, unlike like the time in New Zealand, hiking Mount Cook, when one of the members of the party suffered a stroke. Within the hour, a helicopter arrived and flew him to the hospital.

There were no rescue parties in this land of mist and sky, and a part of Bob liked it that way. It reminded him of his time in Vietnam, the sense of danger in the air, the sense of self-worth, the sense of living in the moment of a *goddamn* perplexing cause that, for better or worse, was greater than oneself, all the while being uncertain of what the next day held.

There was something strangely appealing about this faraway world, not knowing what tomorrow had in store other than the exertion that would be demanded of his body.

And Bob liked the way the four of them walked in silence, as though there was a tacit understanding: in the silence of the mountain, there is much you can learn.

Yachay perpetuated this code of silence. The few times he had communicated with Rudy since departure were a lift of the chin or a subtle gesture with a hand—*this is the way.* He gave off the aura of a man at peace in the silence of his mountain, a man on a mission.

CHAPTER

14

After Bob said, "Hanging in there," in a spirited but a weary tone, Rudy said, "We eat now."

Yachay, who spoke no English, seemed to understand the tonal inflections and pointed to a stony clearing of bunch grass that reminded Devon of clusters of wild straw. Yachay moved his index finger in a circle, indicating his choice of seating arrangements. It seemed to Devon that Yachay liked to communicate with not only his hands but facial gestures as well: a look here, a look there, a brow raised, a brow lowered, the eyes a long slit of concentration, the eyes wide with appreciation of all around him in this land of big sky and mountain. He was speaking a silent, coded language.

As Rudy was handing out the food, Devon decided to take a chance. "Yachay—Padura?" He tapped his heart and made a face. *How is he?*

Yachay took a thoughtful chew on his jerky, his dark eyes on Devon. He nodded okay, pointing to Devon and then bringing it over his heart. "Ayllu."

Rudy said, "He is good but misses his family."

"Agradiseyki," Devon said to Yachay.

Once again, they ate raw quinoa and beef jerky. It was a bland meal, but the combination of dry meat and quinoa seemed to offer plenty of nutritional value, as hunger had not been a problem to this point, though Devon was sore from head to toe.

During the meal, the conversation was at a minimum, Rudy and Yachay discussing the route ahead. Rudy told Devon and Bob their goal was to reach a cave that would provide good shelter.

By late afternoon, they crossed a creek bed over a series of stepping-stones. They walked upstream single file—Yachay in front, Rudy at the rear. They were in a deep-walled gorge. There were some scrubby trees and vine-like plants growing along the hillside on their left; to their right was a steep, rocky wall running the length of the stream that was widening and with a stronger current.

Devon felt that he could use another coca leaf but didn't want to ask. In fact, the only time he or any of them had spoken was during the meal, but it was a comfortable silence, without tension and with an understanding of silent unity.

As they progressed along the side of the stream, it continued to widen, with strong rapids cascading off the side of the canyon walls. Farther on, they turned away from the water and up a zigzagging trail, which was wide enough to walk two by two.

For two hours, they climbed, until finally they reached a level trail running parallel with the stream and a view of the mountains in the distance. Everywhere there were mountains.

Bob asked, "Rudy, can we rest a moment?"

Devon was relieved that Bob had asked. He was pooped. Not only was every muscle in his body screaming, but his lungs couldn't seem to get enough oxygen.

They sat in a row, with their backs to a sheer of rock, overlooking the water caroming recklessly into the rocky sides, creating a repetitive scene of organized chaos. Overhead, the sky was a pale, stark blue, the thin air dry and brisk but reasonably comfortable.

Yachay showed two fingers to Rudy, made a circle with his finger around the palm of his other hand, and then made a walking motion with his fingers.

"Two hours to the cave," Rudy said as he leaned forward, inspecting the two Americans. A smile creased his lips. "Coca leaf, amigos?"

"Ha," Bob said with a lift in his voice, "I thought you'd never ask."

"That is the spirit, Roberto."

Back on the trail, with coca and lime swelling their cheeks, onward they walked. The coca leaf not only alleviated Devon's physical discomfort and breathing, but it offered his spirit a lift.

And it appeared it did so for Bob's as well. The good doctor was walking with purposeful strides, taking it all in with an expression of determined grit.

Devon had always thought of Bob Goodman as a unique person, not only for his world travels but for his *seize the day* outlook on life. But for him to traverse this great mountain at his age was something to behold. He figured they had already walked up and down this mountain a good twenty miles. So, if Bob could continue on, and without a whimper of complaint, then Devon would do his damnedest to follow suit.

While the physical exertion of this trek took its toll on Devon, it also slackened his worry about his father. What would his state of mind be? Would he resist leaving the village? Would the shaman put a curse on all of them? All of those frets had been put on a back burner, for climbing this mountainous beast took every ounce of physical and mental strength Devon could muster out of his twenty-two-year-old being.

By the time they turned off the main trail, it was early evening. The sun was sinking below a reddish-purple horizon. How hauntingly beautiful.

They headed through a short, narrow gully into a meadow of scrub trees and rubble, then to another longer gully, and then up a winding trail until they reached a recess into the side of the rocky hill.

Inside, the ceiling was blackened with soot, and the walls were decorated with carvings of handprints in no discernible pattern. The space was approximately twenty feet in width and depth—plenty of room for all four to stretch out to sleep. Along a wall was a shelf of rock three feet off the floor that made a perfect storage spot for backpacks.

Devon was exhausted, his mind a muddled haze; all he craved was to curl up in his sleeping bag and sleep. But he knew he must eat, which they did sitting in a circle in the middle of the space. It was an effort for Devon to chew the jerky and raw quinoa, his jaw fighting every bite and swallow.

Again, conversation was kept to a minimum, Bob inquiring about the distance to the village—two more days—and Rudy asking, "Roberto, Devon, how are you two amigos holding up?"

"Sore ... tired," Bob said, not complaining, just stating the facts. "But," he went on in an affirmative voice, "nothing a good night's sleep won't fix."

Rudy turned to Devon with a question in his eyes. "Devon?"

"Tired," Devon said, "very tired." He wanted to sound more upbeat, but he could barely mange to get the words out.

Yachay lifted his chin toward Devon. "Puñuy, mas atillcha," he said as his eyes drifted over to Devon's sleeping bag stretched out against a wall.

Yachay then spoke to Rudy in a short burst.

Rudy said, "Yachay says you need rest." He paused and looked at Yachay, who nodded as though he understood. "He also says as that as the son of Padura, the strength of the mountain will grow inside you."

Devon did not awaken until he felt a firm tap on his shoulder and heard a faraway voice saying his name.

Devon rolled over on his back and rubbed the sleep from his eyes. He looked up to find Bob standing over him.

"Morning," Bob said.

"Hey," Devon said sleepily as he began to take stock of himself. He sat up for a moment and then stood. His body was creaky and stiff, but the sound sleep had done wonders for his fatigue.

"Carpe diem?" Bob said through a grin, which crinkled the corners of his eyes on his ruddy, weathered face that had a three-day growth of white stubble.

"Absolutely," Devon replied. "Let us seize this day for all it's worth."

After they ate, they slung on their backpacks and headed out of the cave with cheeks swelled with coca leaf and lime. The air was cold but promised warmth as the day progressed.

Off in the distance, the sun rose between a pair of white-capped mountains that brought to mind pyramids. Devon was sore all over, but his mind was clear and refreshed. Soon, the coca lessened the soreness, and a pleasantness came over him as they passed through a gully and got back on the main trail.

The trail began a slow incline upward, zigzagging one way and then another. The stream was now a good three hundred feet below them.

At last, they reached level ground. Yachay guided them back toward the water. At the edge of the gorge, there was a sheer drop-off as though a giant had chiseled a V into the heart of the mountain. Fifty feet across the water, the stringy remains of a bridge of vines hung down from the other side, bringing to mind a hangman's noose.

Yachay pointed to the cascading water down below. "Aldo wañu."

No one needed translation. This was where Peter Richards had witnessed Aldo Coreas fall to his death.

Devon glanced at Rudy, who was looking down below, where he had discovered Aldo's body. His expression was cold and wounded, as if he were reliving the moment eight years ago all over again.

Devon started to say—but then thought better—that if the bridge had been up, they would have saved much time and many miles, for he guessed the fork in the trail was not far from the other side.

Devon imagined his father crossing the bridge of maguey vines on his way to the shaman. It must have been a scary walk, wobbling his way across with a three-hundred-foot drop below. He couldn't even imagine what his father must have felt on the way down the mountain when he witnessed his guide's fall to death. Not only did he lose his companion, but he was out there alone and unsure and most certainly shaken to the core. This was a land to never let one's guard down. It was important to remain vigilant at all times. If an experienced man like Aldo Coreas could succumb …

Rudy looked up from the bottom of the gorge, staring blankly across to the other side. "Come," he said with a lift in his voice. "Let us walk away from here, and then we eat."

As they walked off, Yachay spoke to Rudy, who then said, "If we go hard today, we can make it to Yachay's abode."

"What do you say, Dr. Goodman?" Devon said.

"Let us eat, amigos," Bob said, "and get us to Yachay's casa *en el cielo*."

Yachay shot a look at Bob and said with a rise in his voice, "Yah." He then tapped his fist over his heart.

The trail led to a series of switchbacks. The first was wide enough for two men to walk side by side, but Devon stayed to Bob's rear, hugging the mountainside, keeping his distance from the cliff to his right. Far below was a stream with a hut nearby. This was their starting point. It was like a miniature scene with the brown land and silvery stream cutting through it, Rudy's SUV looking like a toy.

"Look," Devon said.

"El condor could soar down there in a matter of minutes," Rudy said as they continued to walk.

"Yah," Yachay said with confirmation. "El condor kay qhapaq." (The condor is king.)

Sore as he was, Devon felt as though he was approaching a threshold. In two days, the most painful physical part of the journey would be over, but what remained could be a more difficult challenge—convincing his father to join them and everyone getting safely down the mountain.

Zigzagging one way then the other, slowly but surely, they gained altitude. The top switchback led them to a narrow trail that came to a flat rock surface overlooking a stunning blue lake. A sheer of rock was on one side, and the other was a low area that reminded Devon of a little rocky beach.

"Qhusi Qucha," Yachay said as he gaze settled on the water.

They walked around to the beach. At the water's edge, they splashed their faces and filled their canteens.

At the far end of the lake, they continued through a narrow rock-walled opening. Around a bend, then down a scree, they came to a meadow hundreds of yards long, blanketed by pale-green grass and yellow flowers. Scattered about the meadow were plants that somewhat resembled cacti but were taller—up to twenty feet—and with spiny green leaves recurving in a tightly wound spiral. There was something otherworldly about these beautiful yet odd-looking spires.

"Ah," Rudy said as he fell back to walk with Devon and Bob, "the Puya raimondii—the queen of the Andes. These plants should not grow at such a high altitude or these flowers." He shrugged as they continued walking. "We are most certainly in the land of Cloud People." He shrugged again, as if to say, *It is what it is,* and increased his pace until he caught up with Yachay.

At the meadow's far end was a corral approximately two hundred feet long and half as wide, with a four-foot-high stone wall around the outer edge. Inside were a pair of goats and four llamas. Past the corral, built into the side of the hill, was a stone facade centered by a wood-planked door.

"Is that it?" Devon said.

"Yes," Rudy said, "and with the magnificent llamas." He pointed toward the animals.

As they came along the corral, the llamas stretched their long, curved necks and looked up at them with large doe-like eyes, their pointed ears on high alert. They were unique, regal-looking animals at home in a unique and regal land. Three were grazing on the grass, while one walked the perimeter as if on sentry duty. Two were white and black, one was gray, and the one on sentry duty, the biggest, was reddish tan.

The door in the hillside opened, and a young man similar in age to Devon emerged. He was wearing a collarless, tan, cloth shirt, knee-length trousers, and leather sandals. His jet-black hair was nearly to his shoulders, and his face, the color of polished mahogany, radiated good health. He was strikingly handsome.

Yachay cupped his hands over his mouth and said, "Rimaykullayki, Tian."

The young man raised his hand and made a beeline toward them.

Past a corral gate made of rough-cut timber poles slotted into posts on both ends, Yachay embraced the young man. He then turned to the other men. "Absalón wawáy, Tian" (My son, Tian), Yachay said, his eyes awash in reflexive pride.

Rudy made introductions all around, and hands were shaken and shoulders clasped. Yachay then spoke to Tian, and Devon understood that he was telling him who they were and what their mission was.

"Allin," Tian said as he tapped his heart with his fist.

Tian's welcoming expression turned somber, as did the timbre of his words, as he spoke to his father.

Yachay listened intently, his lower lip thrust out and a trace of tension around his eyes before he seemed to collect himself.

When Tian finished speaking, Yachay nodded. "Yah," he said in a strong, guttural voice.

Tian and Yachay turned to Rudy, their eyes telling him to translate.

Rudy said, "The shaman has died."

"That's good, right?" Devon said.

"It appears we have come at a good time for a rescue," Rudy replied.

"Awgg," Yachay said with a raised hand. He spoke rapid-fire to Rudy in an onslaught of consonant-heavy words with a pronounced stress on the penultimate syllables, and Tian nodded in agreement. Yachay was now speaking with expansive hand gestures. When he finished, he nodded once at Rudy, as if to say, *That is all.*

"He says even though dead, the shaman's power is still potent."

Yachay cleared his throat as if to indicate, *New subject.* He waved them toward the hut. "Chicha," he said in a welcoming tone.

Bob and Devon exchanged knowing smiles.

CHAPTER

15

Yachay and Tian's living quarters were crude—a cavity in the side of a hill encompassed by natural walls of hard earth and stone. One side was empty, other than two bedrolls and blankets. In the middle of the space were two chairs and a roughly made, log-framed table. Nestled in a corner were bulging burlap sacks that Bob figured to contain grain. On a side wall, timber shelves stored earthenware bowls, pots, and cups, their painted surfaces decorated by rows of squares or triangles, repeated one within the other, crosshatching.

On the floor below the shelves was a large, flat stone that served as a preparation table, where Tian, kneeling, poured a pale-yellow liquid from a pot into cups.

"Kuraq samay, Roberto," Tian said to Bob, lifting his chin toward the table and chairs.

"As the senior person," Rudy said, "Tian wants you to sit in a chair."

Bob's first instinct was to ask for no special treatment, but he had been in enough foreign cultures to know it would be rude to decline. "Agradiseyki," he said as he pulled back a chair.

Yachay and Tian brought the grain sacks over to the table, and Yachay then leaned his head toward Rudy and said, "Tiyana."

Rudy sat in the remaining chair, and then the rest of the men sat on the sacks stacked double.

"Huk minutu," Tian said, rising. He went to a shelf and returned with a bowl of caramel-colored powder.

"Maca," Yachay said, as Tian dipped a wooden spoon into the powder and then a spoonful into each cup. He then stirred his drink and passed the spoon around.

"Maca," Rudy said as he handed the spoon back to Tian, "is a root with …" He raised his hand as though searching for the right words. "It is superfood. It will help with our endurance and"—he tapped his temple—"our mental outlook."

Bob took a sip and nearly gagged on the lukewarm liquid. The combination of chicha and maca was bitter and harsh tasting. He looked at Devon, who grimaced down a swallow.

Yachay eyed Bob with an inquisitive look that said, *You like our chicha?* "Qurpa allin," Yachay said through a grin.

Bob took a longer swallow, grimacing, and then said, "Chicha allin." (Chicha good.) At least he hoped that was what he was saying.

Yachay laughed—a robust laugh, a laugh among friends. "Ha, ha, ha." Then Tian followed suit. Soon, all five men were laughing, Bob having to wipe a tear from his eye.

After they finished the chicha, Rudy, Tian, and Yachay had a powwow. The names Attu and Padura were bandied about. Bob assumed they were discussing a plan to extricate Peter from the village.

After they finished talking, Rudy told Bob and Devon that two nights ago, hours before he died, the shaman, knowing his death was imminent, had summoned Peter to his hut. Attu had put a *wañu ñakay* (death curse) on Peter. If he tried to leave the village, he would meet with death, as would anyone who helped him leave. Rudy went on to say that after the shaman died, Tian had offered to guide Peter down the mountain, but he refused. "He will not be responsible for another person's death."

"I will not leave this mountain without my father." Devon's tone was matter-of-fact, but there was a glint in his eyes that Bob had never seen. It was a look Bob had seen in Peter's eyes the day before he left for Peru, a look that said, *I am all in—no turning back.*

CHAPTER

16

Devon's words had surprised him. But he meant them, and by the look on the other men's faces, they were all in agreement.

Tian spoke in a low, steady voice to Rudy. He kept his hands on the table, using his eyes to emphasize a point. He tapped his fist on his chest and concluded by saying, "Attu mana allin." (Attu was a bad man.)

"Tian says the shaman exiled him and his father from the village, and it is their honor and duty to help Padura down the mountain and back to his previous life." Rudy nodded firmly and looked at Yachay, who nodded back. "By breaking the curse, they can then return to the village." Rudy made a walking motion with his fingers. "Chanpuy wasi."

"Yah," Yachay and Tian said in unison.

"But we must be careful," Rudy said as he lifted his brow toward Devon, "for the curse is real."

"Ñakay sinchi," Yachay said. (The curse is strong.) He added that the curse could affect one's body and mind.

Devon wasn't sure what to believe in regard to the curse, but he saw the certainty of belief in the eyes of Yachay and Tian and Rudy. With Bob, he wasn't sure, but it wouldn't surprise him if he at least thought it a strong possibility. And, of course, from what he had heard, no one believed in the curse more strongly than his father.

"We must be vigilant," Rudy said. He pointed toward Devon. "How do we convince your father to leave with us?"

"I think," Bob said, "that when he sees Devon, his paternal instincts will kick in, to the point where he will strongly consider departing the village with us."

"I think first things first," Devon said. "Let us first get to the village."

As they finished their tea, the five men turned inside themselves in a mood of conversational silence, musing wordlessly about what they had discussed and what challenges lay ahead. It reminded Devon of stargazing on a campout with his father; before turning in, father and son would sit in front of the campfire in silence, both absorbing what they had seen in the night sky and experienced together.

At the time, he had taken for granted those magical moments. Yes, those had been special, but there would always be the next time and the time after that. The disappearance of his father had taught Devon to expect the unexpected.

Yachay broke the silence, telling Rudy they should rest while he and Tian prepared dinner. "Let us help," Bob said to Rudy.

"Absolutely," Devon added.

So it was that Bob assisted Yachay inside the hut, and Devon and Rudy helped Tian collect llama dung from the pasture.

The llamas clustered along the fence, as though wary of the two strangers in the middle of the pasture. The reddish-tan one, his long neck raised, clucked aggressively, spreading the racket to the other three. "No," Tian said as he approached the llamas, clicking his tongue off the side of his mouth in rapid, repetitive clicks like a tumbler on a safe. "Allin," he said as he stroked the neck of one llama, then another.

While Tian calmed the llamas, Devon picked up a dark-green dung that was hard and dry and shaped like an oblong egg.

"Reminds me of an Easter egg hunt," he said as he turned it in his hand for closer inspection.

"Hah, you would not want to eat these green eggs," Rudy said as he bent down and picked one up, plopping it in a woven sack before offering the sack to Devon, who made a deposit.

"No," Devon said as he watched Tian soothing the llamas, whispering in their ears, stroking their necks. "It's different here," he said in a changed tone.

Devon looked off toward the meadow, the Puya raimondii plants spiraling above the land like lords surveying their realm. "Not just this intriguing beautiful land but almost as if there is something in the air, a different world aura."

The llamas had settled down, though one let out a final, mournful bleat, *waaa*.

"Yes," Rudy said as he saw Tian approaching, "and with a different set of rules."

"Llama," Tian said, his eyes grinning. He spoke to Rudy as the grin spread to the corner of his mouth.

"He says that when your father collected the dung," Rudy said in a bemused tone, "they had a much bigger herd, and the leader spat in his face."

Devon looked at Tian, his eyes saying, *Really?*

Tian smiled *yes* and then spoke to Rudy, who laughed.

"At first, your father was shocked, but then Tian began to laugh, and soon they were both laughing, hands on knees."

"Padura qhari allin," Tian said with a nod of affirmation. (Padura good man.)

"No translation needed, Rudy," Devon said.

Dinner was a treat. Tian cooked a potato goulash dish over hot coals of the llama dung and scraps of wood from scrub trees on the hillside that Bob had collected. They also had boiled quinoa and goat meat cooked on wood skewers. Devon thought it all delicious after raw quinoa and jerky.

They ate in silence as though they had used up their limit of words for the day, and a tacit sense of purpose came over the group. There seemed an understanding of what the job ahead was: get to the village and then somehow convince Peter Richards to depart with them. Devon could not imagine his father refusing. But how much had he changed? All these years living in a remote Quechua village could change a man—change his priorities. Maybe, in a way, his dad was comfortable as the great Padura in a confined life of mountain and sky. Maybe he liked that he didn't have to worry about a mortgage, or his architectural firm, or traffic, or who knew what. Maybe his father was no longer the man he used to be.

After dinner, they all turned in, nestled in their sleeping bags and bedrolls under the soft light of two wall torches flickering muted light across the hut.

In the middle of the night, Devon woke with a start. He had dreamt that he had entered a village of adobe huts that blurred together to form a silvery arc. Inside the arc was his father, wearing the same red poncho as in the other dream, and again he had a beard and ponytail. It was his father, and it wasn't his father, as though Peter Richards had morphed into a strange and different version of the man who had raised Devon.

There was a beautiful, bronze-skinned woman with glowing black hair at Peter's side, dressed in a green patterned shawl and embroidered skirt. In between Peter and the woman was a ten-year-old boy wearing sandals, shin-length trousers, and a shiny blue poncho. The boy possessed his mother's beauty and Peter's eyes, dark brown and knowing. All three of their faces said, "Leave us. You are not welcome."

To see his father like that, with other people his dad now considered his family, was crushing. Even though it was only a dream, Devon began to wonder—dare he think it—if it was part of the curse. Maybe the shaman, from the afterlife, had somehow transmitted this dream to him, to shake him up, to cause him to lose sleep and possibly affect his stamina in the days to come.

Devon snuggled into his sleeping bag, and as he drifted off to sleep, he thought about stargazing in the backyard with his father when they returned home, just the two of them, just like it was when he was a boy—father and son with a bond no entity of this earth could break.

CHAPTER

17

At sunrise, they ate raw quinoa and cold potato goulash left over from the previous night, and each man downed a cup of maca powder in water.

Making their way up the hillside behind the hut, Devon sucked on his wad of coca leaf. Combined with the maca, he did feel refreshed, and his body, though still sore, felt prepared to take on the challenges ahead.

Yachay and Tian led the group, with Devon and Bob behind and Rudy pulling up the rear. The sky, which had been clear since they embarked up the mountain, was crammed with dark, threatening clouds shrouding the mountains in the distance. The air had a chilly bite to it and a scent of snow—a scent of change.

Devon had a sudden vision of his mother, her expression that of distressed worry. Debra Richards was at the kitchen sink, looking out the back window at the ten-foot-high platform in the middle of the backyard. A surge of guilt rushed through Devon; he had barely thought about his mother since he left Portland.

Devon looked upon his life up to graduating college as in two phases: with his father and mother and with only his mother. During both phases, Debra Richards had been the quiet, efficient parent. She had always scheduled meetings with teachers, when needed, drove Devon to friends' houses or school functions, and looked after Devon's schoolwork and grades.

When Devon had a difficult transition into ninth grade, losing friends from middle school who suddenly considered him too nerdy for their taste, he became a lonely, sullen boy whose grades dropped precipitously. All this had transpired during Peter's funk from his brain cancer. Without his mother's vigilance, Devon wasn't sure where he would be.

When Peter departed for Peru, Debra encouraged Devon to join the astronomy club at school and then to invite boys from the club over to the house and the observation deck. Soon, Devon had a new group of friends, with overnight campouts in the backyard and stargazing on the observation deck.

As Devon's personal life returned to an even keel, his grades rose back to the honor roll. But both Devon's and his mother's life had a huge vacuum in regard to the whereabouts of Peter.

After a year of no word on Peter, they both settled into a routine that on the outside appeared to be a normal life. Devon's included school, stargazing, and, by junior year, girls. For Debra, it was gardening, socializing with the wives of Peter's business partners, and volunteer work at the Red Cross. Devon once overheard Debra tell a friend on the phone that without her three days a week at the Red Cross, she didn't know where she would be. Her voice had a mixed tone of relief and trepidation—relief for the volunteer work and trepidation for her lost/dead husband.

In the years since Devon's father's disappearance, Debra never broached the subject with Devon. The first time they discussed it was when Devon said that he and Bob were going to Peru to find an answer. Devon realized that to most people that would seem weird, but what was there to talk about? They didn't know what had happened to Peter, and bringing it up would only throw salt on an open wound.

From this other world of mountain and sky, looking back on his life with one parent, Devon realized how much his mother had sacrificed for him—not just in always being there for him but also putting her life on hold while his progressed forward.

His mother was like a wobbly planet that needed to be brought back to its proper rotational axis. Bringing his dad back would provide the Richards family universe its proper alignment.

As the first snow began to fall, they wove their way through a narrow pass and then up a steep trail that led to a stretch of level ground before another upward climb. Not a word had been spoken since they left the hut. The snow was now coming down in swirling gusts, making not only visibility difficult but also the simple act of walking. Rudy walked up to the front and spoke with Yachay and Tian.

"There's a recess in the mountain not far ahead," Rudy said over his shoulder. "We will stop and wait."

"Okay," Bob said. His voice was taut and tense, as though a cord had been pulled tight inside his larynx.

As they continued on, Bob began to walk with a slight limp. The look of one on a great adventure had been replaced by that of struggle and strain.

By the time they came to the recess, the snow had relented to flurries, but Bob's limp had worsened so that he was nearly dragging his right leg.

The recess was an alcove that opened enough into the rocky hillside to give the men shelter from the elements. They were at the edge of a meadow of scrub trees and rubble. It was a lonely, desolate place.

They sat in a circle, Bob's problem leg extended, and ate raw quinoa and jerky. "How are you doing, Roberto?" Rudy's question was the first mention of Bob's struggle.

Bob took a swig of water from his canteen and wiped his mouth with his forefinger. "Cramp in my thigh—first I've ever had."

Yachay spoke in a strong, defiant voice. He made a fist and then pointed to the middle of the circle.

They all clasped hands. "Ñuqayku sinchi," Yachay said.

"Together, we are strong," Rudy translated.

"Yes, amigos," Bob said. "Ñu … qay … ku … sin … chi," he said in a firm, deliberate voice.

With cheeks packed with lime and coca, they left the recess with renewed confidence. There had been a veil of anguish hanging over Devon and Bob and possibly the others. It was as though the curse had seeped into Bob's body and Devon's psyche. But the clasping of hands and Yachay's words—Ñuqayku sinchi—had initiated a charged air of togetherness among them. *Together we are strong.*

The touching of hands and Yachay's words, even before Devon knew the meaning, delivered a force field of kinetic energy surging through him and with it an unexplainable connection of oneness with his comrades.

The whole is greater than the sum of the parts, Devon thought as he observed Bob moving without a limp as they passed through a patch of barren land littered with rocks, boulders, and scrub trees. They silently pushed forward, five men unified on a mission, five men from different corners of the world working as one.

At dusk, they came to a series of steps that led down to the ruins of a village. Below them, stone walls weaved around stone huts in no discernible pattern. Pointy-topped rock formations rose up at the promontory's edge, beyond which the fading sunlight peeked out between brown-green mountains, their peaks veiled by misty clouds.

Down the steps they walked around the ramparts, with a terrace of wild grass sticking up through a topping of snow. They trudged up another set of steps to an arched opening into the side of the mountain. The alcove was a tight fit for the men, but it provided cover from the cold air and intermittent snow. After stacking their gear in a corner, they sat in a circle and ate bread, raw quinoa, and jerky, then washed everything down with a spoonful of maca and a swig of water. Devon was tuckered out, as was Bob. The others seemed none the worse for wear.

After eating, Rudy said, "Tomorrow, if all goes well, we should reach the village by noon."

Devon looked at Bob. It seemed to hit them both. *This may actually happen—meeting Dad/Peter.*

"Now that we don't have to contend with the shaman in the village, we should discuss how to approach Peter," Bob said.

Tian and Yachay were listening, seeming to decipher the words through body language.

"Bob," Devon said, "I think you and Rudy should approach my father. Seeing me first might come as too much of a shock." Devon was concerned about his father's frightened reaction to seeing him in his nightmares. He looked at Bob and then Rudy. *What do you think?*

Rudy spoke to Yachay and Tian in a short, guttural burst of words. They both nodded okay.

CHAPTER

18

At dawn, they headed back up the mountain, the air brisk but tolerable, the snow from yesterday now only a dusting. Devon's muscles were still sore, but even more than that, they were tight—like when his body tensed up in preparation for finals. He imagined the cause was the anticipation of seeing his father. He was determined to keep up with Yachay and Tian, who were moving at a strong pace, like hunting dogs following a scent.

An hour into the trek, Bob asked them to stop. He put his hand over his heart. "I have a rapid pulse," he said as he brought his forefinger to his nose, trickling blood. "Awgg." He grunted in disgust.

They were in a scrubby meadow. Up ahead was a steep-sided gully, and in the distance were the inscrutable mountains.

Tian cleared a dusting of snow off a large, flat rock.

Bob sat and looked at his hands that had swelled; his long, lean fingers looked distortedly stubby. "Altitude sickness. Another first." Bob shook his head and sighed. He took a drink of water, looked off for a moment, and said, "I know the signs. I know the symptoms. I don't think it's safe for me to climb any higher."

Rudy powwowed with Tian and Yachay. "Yachay will stay here with you and later take you back to the ruins. We will meet you on the way down the mountain."

Bob didn't say anything for a moment before a defiant look came over him: the eyes steady and sure, the mouth drawn together in a thin, determined line. He extended his hands to the others, who locked hands in a circle.

They said in unison, "Ñuqayku sinchi."

Walking without Bob felt strange to Devon. Now Rudy was at his side, with Tian in the lead. He wondered why Bob, who had been in high altitude before, had gotten altitude sickness but not him. He remembered Yachay's words: "As the son of Padura, the strength of the mountain will grow inside you."

After a couple of hours, they came to a path off the trail that led to a terraced stone corral with llamas and goats—close to a hundred in all—grazing on moss-green grass. At the far end of the corral were three lean-to shelters equally spaced apart, thirty feet or more.

"We must be getting close," Devon said to Rudy, who only nodded, his eyes busy in thought.

The trail wound around a bend. Off to their right, a wide and half as deep terraced hillside with a series of earth-and-timber steps descended to a patch of level ground before a sheer drop-off overlooking a valley far below. A variety of leafy crops were growing in neatly spaced rows all the way down the hillside. Villagers were digging out of the ground, with wooden trowels, strangely shaped tubers colored red, yellow, purple, even candy striped, some as round and bright as billiard balls, others oblong. Placed at intervals along the rows were handwoven reed baskets to collect their yield.

A couple more steps, and the village came into view, situated on a jut of rock and hard earth. To their left, thatched-roofed adobe huts lined the perimeter in a half-moon arc, similar to the shape of the blurry village in Devon's dream. But this was no dream. This was reality. Somewhere in there was his father! He had to get a grip on himself and also figure out how his father should be approached now that Bob was not with them.

The three men stood there waiting until Rudy said, "Maybe Tian should talk with your father first?"

"No, Rudy." Devon had the strongest sense that he must meet his father. That he must challenge his dreams. That he must not be afraid. "I think it best if I go with him."

"Yah," Tian said, as he seemed to decipher through Devon's tone. He gestured for them to follow him.

They passed a few villagers, who stopped and gaped at Tian with the two strangers. One man approached Tian, blocking his path. The man was in his fifties, dressed in a collarless brown shirt and sandals. There was something unnerving and obsequious about this short brown man with stooped shoulders and sly, probing eyes.

"Quien?" The man said to Tian as he lifted his chin in the direction of Devon and Rudy.

Tian spoke with his eyes that said, *I will not be deterred.*

"Ven para Padura?" The man said in an accusatory tone.

"Yah, Rumi."

"Mana," Rumi said, his dark eyes two angry slits. He then extended his arms, pushing his hands into Tian's chest. "Ripuy!" he said as he gestured with his hands in a short, sweeping motion for them to depart the village.

Tian continued to speak with his eyes.

Rumi spoke to Tian in a short, rapid burst, his dark eyes saying, *No!*

Villagers began to come over, drawn to the ruckus. They were dressed simply in collarless shirts, ponchos, and knee-length trousers, a few of the older women in brightly colored skirts with zigzag patterns.

Rumi began talking to the crowd in a strong, resistant voice.

A heavyset woman dressed in a faded blue shirt, rolled up to the elbows, and knee trousers approached Tian. She wore her dark hair in pigtails, and her skin was a creamy caramel hue that was accentuated by a smile that revealed the pretty girl she once was.

"Y wawa," she said to Tian, who had not noticed her in his stare down with Rumi.

"Mama," Tian said as they embraced for a moment. Tian then spoke to his mother, pointing at Devon and Rudy. He seemed to be explaining who they were.

Tian's mother turned to Rumi and spoke sharply with her finger wagging.

She was like a scolding parent. Back and forth it went, Rumi speaking with forceful passion and then Tian's mother.

All the while, Devon wondered where his father was.

During a pause, Rudy said to Tian's mother, "May Padura?"

All eyes turned to Rudy.

"Mana," Rumi said.

Tian's mother flicked her hand at Rumi as if he were an annoying fly. She then proceeded to speak with Rudy.

Rudy said to Devon, "After the shaman's death, the villager asked your father to go off on his own and ask Viracocha, the mountain god, for guidance."

"When is he expected back?"

"Soon," Rudy said with glance and a quick smile at Tian's mother. "They are having a big powwow this evening, and he is expected back for it."

Tian waved them over to an open-air thatched-roof structure supported by timber poles and a back wall made of straw and mud. In the middle was a high-legged table, behind which was a cluster of earthenware pots, each strung from a wooden tripod over hot coals. Along the back wall were bags of grain and wicker baskets brimming with potatoes and the colorful tubers.

They sat at a long, rough-hewn table along the outer edge of the cooking hut. The seats and backs of the wood-framed chairs were made of tightly woven vines. Tian's mother came over and placed her finger on her chest. "Mariaqua." She made a face to Rudy—*your turn.*

Rudy introduced himself and Devon.

Mariaqua smiled and said something to Tian. She would prepare food for them.

So many things were racing through Devon's mind: Would the villagers offer resistance to his father leaving? Would his father want to leave? What would his father look like—old and gray, worn out from living high in this mountain village? And would he have changed completely from the man Devon knew and loved?

Mariaqua and a younger woman, slender with long jet-black hair, served hot potato soup, flatbread, and a platter piled high with succulent goat meat. The smell and flavor were wonderful, but Devon's appetite was stymied by his anxiety. He was excitedly nervous in anticipation of seeing his father walk into the village.

Over the meal, Rudy and Tian spoke at length. The gist of it was that the powwow would be held in the middle of the village square and would be led by Rumi, who had been the shaman's second in command.

The main objective was to name a new chief of the village. Attu had been chief and shaman, unusual in Quechua culture. But whoever it was, there was no shaman-in-waiting. Attu had not groomed anyone for the position that was normally separate from tribal leader. But years ago, Attu had run off the leader, who was his brother and Yachay's father.

The two leading candidates for leader were Rumi and Peter, who Tian said would grudgingly take the position, since he didn't want Rumi in charge.

Mariaqua led the newcomers to her hut, where they could wait until the powwow. It was a basic structure with two windows in the front with rawhide flaps rolled up and tied above. Reed mats and blankets sat on opposite sides of the space, and stationed above each mat was a torch in a dadoed slot in the wall. A table with two chairs was in a corner, and that was it.

"Rudy, you and Tian get some rest," Devon said as he pointed toward the wood-planked door. "I am going to be on the lookout for my father's arrival."

Rudy exchanged a quick look with Tian, who nodded his head slightly. "We will wait with you, amigo."

CHAPTER

19

Resting on the flat rock off the trail, Bob looked up at Yachay, who was standing over him with an intense look—a lift of the brow, a nod, a knowing pursing of the lips.

"Hampi," Yachay said. He raised a finger to indicate he had an idea.

Yachay extended his tongue, indicating for Bob to do the same. He then pinched his fingers into a leather pouch attached to a belt loop by a lace of rawhide. He put a dab of maca powder on the tip of Bob's tongue, followed by a swig of water. "Hampina," Yachay said as he continued to administer his remedy.

Afterward, Yachay went off and returned with some sticks and dry, weedy grass and a round stone with a deep recess, like a stone bowl. He balled up the dry grass on the flat rock and placed the sticks over it. He then struck a spark with a blade of flint, and soon a small fire was lit. He removed another pouch from a belt loop; he had three pouches in all. "Ayahuasca," he said as he poured a dark-green liquid from the pouch into the stone's recess.

When the fire died down, Yachay placed the stone over the hot coals for a few minutes. After letting it cool, he handed the stone to Bob and said, "Machay."

Bob was already feeling better from the maca powder, his pulse having returned to normal, but his fingers were still swollen. He took the warm stone and drank the harsh liquid that had an acrid, bitter taste. It was godawful, but he swallowed it down.

"Samay," Yachay said with palm raised.

Bob understood that he wanted him to rest.

After an hour of sitting in silence, a comfortable silence, Yachay lifted his finger as if to say, *One more thing.* "Coca," he said.

By now, Bob felt good. Actually, more than good, he felt rejuvenated. The swelling of his fingers was gone, his breathing was normal, and his body, though sore, felt ready to continue up the mountain. Bob packed the coca and lime in his cheeks and pointed up the mountain.

Yachay nodded his approval and reached for Bob's hand. "Ñuqayku sinchi."

CHAPTER

20

T ian, Rudy, and Devon stood outside Mariaqua's hut, waiting and watching. Tian said that Peter would be coming from down the mountain. He pointed to a trail leading past the far end of the village, past the cooking hut. "Padura chayay."

There was activity in the village square: Mariaqua and another woman were shucking corn at the cooking hut, while two others were skinning a goat carcass hanging by its back legs. Nearby, a large pot of water sat on stacked logs, awaiting ignition. Two other women pounded water-soaked long grass with rounded wooden clubs. One of them then mashed it into a pulp, while the other took it into long strands between her dexterous fingers, no movement wasted.

In the middle of the square, men were preparing wood for a bonfire, first with twigs and dry grass, over which they stacked long logs in a vertical teepee.

With nothing to do but sit and wait, Devon said to Rudy, "Could you ask Tian about my father?"

Tian replied, "Padura k'acha runa." (He is a good man.)

Tian went on to say that Devon's father, as the reincarnate of a great leader, was a respected member of the village. When he first arrived in the village, Attu had a hut built next to his for Padura to live in. Tian lifted his chin toward the largest hut in the village. "Attu wasi." (Attu's abode.) Right next to it was a standard-size hut,

At first, Padura was terribly unhappy—wandering about with a blank expression on his face, barely eating, spending long stretches of the day alone in his hut. But after time, he began to join in the fabric of the village society, helping with planting and harvesting the crops, attending celebrations for the birth of a child or the grand fiesta after harvest.

Attu wanted Padura to marry an eligible woman in the village, but he flatly refused. He said he would die first. Attu relented, and it was never brought up again. For all the while, Padura's heart was elsewhere, and over time, it became apparent that he was not living in the village of Olaquecha but existing. Even so, he would not consider leaving. His near death and the death of Aldo Coreas had affected him greatly.

And the shaman never let him forget, reminding him over the years that if he had never left the village, Aldo Coreas would have been allowed safe passage and still be alive.

The shaman's reason for keeping Peter living in the village became apparent as, year after year, the village had bountiful crops, and the people were in good health, with nary one death until the shaman's. "Padura, hampi yachay." (Padura's presence is big medicine.)

"Yachay?" Devon asked.

Rudy explained that, in Quechua, the word *yachay* had many meanings relating to wisdom and knowledge.

So, not only the shaman but also the villagers believed that Padura's presence was essential. But even with the good crops and good health of the people, the village was out of alignment with the evil Attu acting as leader and shaman. Tian looked upward as long, feathery clouds sailed across the deep-blue sky. "Attu mana allin." (Attu no good.)

Tian spoke to Rudy, emphasizing with his hands.

"Tian says that Yachay was groomed by his father, Havo, the village chief, to replace him upon his death, but Attu—Havo's younger brother—had great power as shaman and used it to turn the people against Havo and Yachay, expelling them from the village.

"Look," Rudy said.

Coming into the village was a man with a bedroll strung across his shoulder, leading a llama loaded with a bundle covered by a blanket. He was of medium height with broad shoulders, wearing a collarless shirt and poncho. He had an unkempt beard with flecks of gray, and his eyes had a downtrodden look. He seemed to be walking by rote, as though going through the motions.

"Oh my God!" Devon said. "It's my father." He looked at Rudy and then stood and moved toward his father.

Peter Richards looked up and blinked as though trying to make sure of what he was seeing. Then he released the reins, dropped to his knees, started to speak, and fell forward into a heap.

CHAPTER

21

Devon rushed over to his father and turned him over. "Dad! Dad!"

"Let's get him in Mariaqua's hut," Rudy said as a crowd gathered around.

"Padura, oh, Padura," a woman cried out. There was a buzz of conversation in the group, and then Rumi arrived. He gave an order, and a group of men began to lift Peter.

"No," Devon said. He bent down and put his arm around his father's shoulder. "No. Mi padre."

Rudy said something to the villagers and then turned to Rumi. "Padura, kay tayta."

Rudy took in the measure of Rumi, his eyes saying, *I will not be deterred.*

Meanwhile, Devon and Tian had lifted Peter up by the shoulders, their other arms under his legs.

Tian gave a command to the crowd, and they began to disperse, save Rumi. He shouted angrily at Tian in a raw vitriol of words.

Ignoring Rumi, Tian and Devon carried the unconscious Peter inside Mariaqua's hut. They placed him down on Devon's sleeping bag.

Devon turned at the sound of the door opening, and there stood Bob with Yachay. "Well, I'll be," Bob said as he recognized

Peter. "I had a feeling I needed to be here." The doctor stepped into the space.

Bob knelt down at Peter's side, checked his pulse on his wrist, then opened Peter's mouth and checked his airways. He then told Devon to raise Peter's legs as he loosened the cord around his pants.

Peter's eyes opened and closed in slow blinks. He stared wide-eyed at Bob as his mouth gaped open. "Kay chiqa?" (Is it true?) His gaze remained on Bob as though trying to assure what he was seeing was real. "Bob? ... Bob?" he said in a low mumble.

"Hello, Peter, my old friend," Bob said.

Peter extended a shaky hand, which Bob held in his.

"Dr. Goodman, I presume," Peter said through a weak smile. "How ... how ..." He turned his attention to Devon. "I thought it was a dream. It is you ... Devon. You're all grown-up."

Peter reached up and put his arm around his son's neck, and Devon knelt forward, burying his face in his father's neck as he felt a swell of emotion rise in his throat, his heart pounding his chest.

Devon breathed in Peter's familiar fatherly scent and something else—something wild and foreign, something instinctually unsettling.

"How's your mother?" Peter asked Devon.

"She misses you, Dad. We never gave up hope that you were alive."

Peter's eyes glistened with tears. "How I missed you both." He looked off for a moment and then back at his son. "I can't—"

Bob cut in, "Let me introduce you to our guide."

Peter extended his arm to Devon. "Help me up, buddy."

All six men sat on the floor in a circle.

"Without this man," Bob said with a nod toward Rudy, "we wouldn't be here."

Peter offered his hand to Rudy. "Agradisikuyki, amigo." He smiled as if mostly to himself. "It seems strange. I haven't spoken English in years." He squinted a nod at his Quechua friends. "Without Yachay and Tian, *I* wouldn't be here today."

He looked around at the group, Tian and Yachay taking it all in, seeming to once again understand the gist of the conversation through body language and voice inflection.

Peter said, "I lost count. How long have I been here?"

"Eight years, Dad."

Bob filled Peter in on how their trek came about, their journey up the mountain, things back home, and world events. "The planet is still in one piece. I'll save the details for later."

Peter told them about his healing by the shaman. "It was an amazing ceremony under the stars, the entire village in attendance. Afterward, I thought I was cured, but my pragmatic side wasn't completely sold." Peter coughed a dry, thirsty cough.

Bob handed him his canteen, and Peter took a few careful sips between throat-clearing small coughs. He handed the canteen back to Bob and said, "The Pleiades are very important in Quechua society." He looked to Devon. "It might explain my fascination with that cluster of stars."

Peter went on to say, "I have experienced enough and seen enough in my time here to know without question that there are things modern science cannot explain." Peter looked at Tian and Yachay sitting next to each other and said, "Kapukiri wayra." (Magic in the air.)

"Ari," they both said in a strong voice of confirmation.

"And," Peter said as he slid a look at Bob, who was observing Peter with rapt attention, part doctor on duty, part friend absorbed in what he was hearing, "it turns out they believe I am the reincarnate—a starman—of a legendary leader, Padura." Peter spread his hands to the circle. "I imagine Tian and Yachay have filled you in on all that." He gave his beard a thoughtful scratch. "It is a lot to comprehend—even for me, and I experienced it firsthand."

Peter mentioned his *chiqap purly* (truth journey) up the mountain. "I was to find the answers for how the village would proceed after the shaman's death." He shook his head and exhaled. "Two days and one night sleeping in a cave, and I had no inspiration at all.

"So different than when I first arrived, where I had a couple of monumental moments of consciousness, as though I had been transported to another dimension. The day after the healing ceremony, still wondering if I was really healed, I went off by myself and sat on a rock with view of a hardscrabble landscape of rock and earth, the view more desolate than from the terraced hillside of green valley. My mind drifted away from its present view into a state that I can only describe as nothingness. It seemed a place where time did not exist, a place unencumbered by the physical world, a place so vague yet so clear.

"I looked out to the mountains in the distance, brown and vague, and lost myself in a semiconscious state, drifting, into a harmonious mind-set of nothingness, an otherworldly place where the senses were useless.

"At dusk, I came out of it. I felt a subdued energy of prescient awareness that told me I was cured. Simply cured."

Peter added, "Ever since that day, I've had no more moments like that, as though my mental receptor has been blocked—Attu's handy work, I imagine."

"How are you feeling, Peter?" Bob asked.

"I'm okay, still a bit in shock from seeing my boy." Peter reached for Devon's hand, his eyes crinkling a smile. "I feel healthy, if lonely until now." He shrugged and said, "Can't help but be healthy living up here on quinoa and oca."

Rudy asked Bob how he got up the mountain. "It didn't look like there was any way you could continue."

"Maca powder, coca leaf, and some other secret potion of Yachay's that had me back on my feet after resting." Bob put his hand on Yachay's shoulder. "Allin runa." (This is wise and good man.)

Yachay offered a modest nod, but his eyes couldn't hide the appreciation of the praise.

"Damn, Bob," Peter said, "you've only been on this mountain a couple days, and you're already learning the language."

"I studied a Quechua dictionary before departure." Bob turned his hands palms up. "Old habit," he said with a shrug.

After some more exchanges about life in Olaquecha and back in Portland, Peter looked at Devon and said in a tone of finality, "I can't leave here, Dev. I will not be responsible for another man's death trying to escape Attu's curse."

"Dad ..." Devon said as he felt a knot tighten in his stomach. He had known he would face this moment, but now, to be in it, with his father saying he wouldn't go back with them hurt so badly.

Peter said, "Attu spared my life and took Aldo's. Lesson learned. I'm not letting his ghost take any of yours."

CHAPTER

22

Devon's hands were trembling at the thought of his father not departing with them. Compounding the issue, his mind was crammed with worry, and to top it off, he felt as though he might throw up. He couldn't imagine going home and telling his mother, "I found Dad alive, but he won't leave the mountain. It's a curse."

Debra Richards would not understand. She was a wonderful and loving mother and wife who had devoted herself to her son and husband. Since Devon's father's absence, she had lived as though in limbo. Holding out a slim chance of hope that her husband was alive, she maintained a stiff upper lip and went on with her life, much like a wife of an MIA.

For Devon to walk back down the mountain without his father and have to break the good news, bad news to his mother was not the ending he wanted. Yes, it was better than the alternative, but in a way, it would be like his father was dead if they couldn't get him home.

What struck Devon when first he saw his father was how much he looked like what he had imagined in his dreams—the hair in a ponytail and the beard flecked with bits of gray. The feedbag beard didn't add any age to his father, though he looked different. There was still an attentiveness and a vigor about him, even in his worn-down state. But at the same time, there was also something different that he had first sensed when he hugged his father—part of it smell, part the tension he felt from his father's touch, and part a feeling of being in the presence of wildness, an atavistic recurrence throwing him back to ancestral form. Padura?

Devon knew he couldn't continue trying to convince his father. His emotions were running too high, and he might say something he regretted. He turned to Bob, hoping the smartest man in the room had an answer for this dilemma.

"Rudy," Bob said as he crossed his legs Indian style and looked around the circle of men, "would you mind translating what I am about to propose?"

Bob suggested that at the village gathering this evening, Peter recommend Yachay as the new tribal leader. "Yachay is the rightful heir," Bob said, as he put his hand on Yachay's shoulder. "Kuaka Qusmi Runa." (Chief of the Cloud People.)

"Arí," Tian said. He then said that it was time for him and his father to take their rightful places back in the village.

"What say tonight, Peter, you tell the village the truth, that you had no vision and, with their blessing, you would like to return home?"

"And," Rudy added, "that Rumi will become Yachay's deputy." Rudy translated to Yachay and Tian.

Tian turned to his father. They looked into each other's eyes. "Yah," they said in unison.

"That's all good, but I don't see how it eliminates the curse," Peter said. "I won't be responsible for another man's death."

"Dad," Devon said in a near plea, "if we are vigilant, we can get back home all in one piece."

Peter sat across from his son, his eyes narrowed slits, his lips pursed.

"I can't go home and tell Mom that I found you but you wouldn't leave."

Bob, sitting next to Peter, took his right hand in his left and firmed his grip. "There comes a time in a man's life where he must dare ... or what is the purpose of it all?"

Bob turned and faced Peter. "Are you with us?"

"I want to be."

"Do you remember a poem I recited to you one evening after horseshoes right after you were diagnosed with cancer?"

Peter straightened, his posture erect. "'Invictus.'"

Bob began reciting, and Peter joined in.

Devon was taken by the growing strength of resistance in his father's voice as he and Bob let the words flow out of their mouths in perfect harmony. It was beautiful to behold.

> Out of the night that covers me,
> Black as the pit from pole to pole,
> I thank whatever gods may be
> For my unconquerable soul.
>
> In the fell clutch of circumstance
> I have not winced nor cried aloud.
> Under the bludgeoning of chance
> My head is bloody, but unbowed.
>
> Beyond this place of wrath and tears
> Looms but the Horror of the shade,
> And yet the menace of the years
> Finds, and shall find me, unafraid.
>
> It matters not how strait the gate,
> How charged with punishments the scroll,
> I am the master of my fate:
> I am the captain of my soul.

When they finished, there was silence, until Peter said, "Let us leave at first light."

CHAPTER

23

After agreeing to depart the village, Peter said he wanted to return to his hut to rest before the big powwow. It was much to comprehend. Bob and Devon had come to Olaquecha to rescue him—a great friend and a great son. How Devon had grown; he was now a tall and well-constructed man. His son, when last he saw him, was bitterly upset with his father for leaving with death knocking at the door. In a way, it seemed a lifetime ago, another life. Here in this small Quechua village, he was Padura, the former great leader of the Quechua people.

After Attu had cured him of the cancer, Peter had a dream of his past life. Padura was a gifted boy whom the elders selected for grooming as Kamachiq (leader), taking him from his mother as soon as he could walk to begin his education.

His young, growing mind sought knowledge about the stars, especially the Pleiades, birthplace of the creator Viracocha and whose location and brightness in the sky were closely followed for not only agrarian purposes but also for deciding important civic and social functions.

Young Padura learned the craft of cutting stone and erecting structures that endured the shaking of the earth when Viracocha was displeased and building tables and chairs that lasted for a thousand years by using only the materials that the trees offered and the secrets of the knotted strings, Khipu.

By the time he had grown tall and strong, he was noticeably larger than the other boys and even the men. Padura was on his way to becoming Kamachiq.

As Kamachiq, Padura took a wife, a black-haired, chiseled beauty, Maya. They had a son, Cusi, who had his father's noble features with an aquiline nose, cleft chin, and hair like dark grain in a gentle breeze. Life was good and the crops bountiful—until the arrival of the tall men with bronze skin, who had traveled across vast waters and walked many days. Their language was in a strange tongue, so they communicated with their hands. They stayed seven days and enjoyed the effects of the coca leaf.

During their visit, the bronze men taught Padura how to store events of the sky with braided ropes, which were like the Khipu but thicker and stronger, and their system for counting that used *ch'usaq* and *huq*—zero and one. This was the first knowledge Padura had ever received beyond the teaching of the elders and the gifted working of his own mind.

Viracocha came to Padura in a dream and warned of consequences of allowing outsiders to live among his people and sleep with the women.

When the first of the illness struck, more than half the villagers found their skin erupted in boils filled with yellowy-white pus, bringing complaints of weakness and sore muscles. Some had spots on their tongues and fell terribly ill.

Padura lost his wife and son and most of his villagers to the pestilence.

Heartbroken from the loss, Padura decided that never again would his people be touched by the disease of the *mana riqsisqa* (strangers).

He went with his *maskhays* on a trek high up the mountain. After much searching, he found a secluded land that would be a difficult journey for any mana riqsisqa. For the remainder of his life, Padura devoted himself to his people, Phuyu Runa—the Cloud People. Over many years, his people's numbers grew. During that time, no strangers had discovered them, nor had any illness struck his people.

Padura left this world just as he had entered. On the night of his death, the seven maidens hid behind the moon and did not appear again for seven nights. It was said that Viracocha forbade them from showing themselves until he had finished mourning. Thus the legend of Padura was passed on for many generations, that someday his spirit would return and never leave the mountain again.

When he awoke from the dream that was as real as any reality, Peter felt torn between a love of his past life as Padura and that as Peter Richards. But a yearning for Debra and Devon overwhelmed everything else, costing Aldo Coreas his life.

When Yachay brought him back to the village, Peter was devastated. Mariaqua nursed him back to health, but Peter's heart and soul ached, not only for Aldo's death—which he felt responsible for—but because he would never see his family again. Attu warned the villagers that anyone helping Padura down the mountain would be met by deadly consequences. Not wanting to be responsible for another death, Peter resigned himself to life as the reincarnate of Padura.

Over time, he began to assimilate into the culture. It was hard not to, for the people were so kind to him. Peter was welcomed in any enterprise he undertook. When he came out to the hillside crops, he was shown the ancient and true growing methods of building irrigation canals and cisterns. This appealed to the architect in him, and he emerged from his depression with an attitude of acceptance. He would make the best of his existence— an existence that he realized would no longer have been if he had not come to Olaquecha. He would surely be dead.

Never far from his mind, though, were his wife and son and the life he had left behind in Portland. He imagined they considered him dead, and as the years went on, he wondered if Debra had remarried and Devon had a new father figure in his life he called Dad.

Debra was a fine-looking woman. Peter had imagined that after a reasonable waiting period, she would draw the attention of other men. She was slender with a lovely face, highlighted by a pinch of pink high in the cheeks, chestnut-colored hair that fell to her shoulders, and wide-set brown eyes that seemed to transmit a certain hospitable warmth.

She and Peter had met at the University of Oregon. It was at a school rally and bonfire for a big football game. When a fight broke out between a couple of fraternities, Debra ended up taking a spill. Peter helped her up and got her away from the turmoil.

He sat her down on a bench and asked if she was okay. When she looked at Peter for the first time, those light-brown eyes so soft and true, Peter knew right then and there, she was the one. It was as though he had been waiting for her all his life.

And now Peter was stuck in this other life. In a way, he considered Peter Richards dead; he was now Padura. As he learned the language and fell into life high in this Andean hideaway, he accepted his fate, though never forgetting who he once was.

Now, all of what he had accepted had been turned upside down by the amazing arrival of Devon and Bob. Reciting "Invictus" with Bob had been cathartic—an awakening of mind and body. As he recited each stanza of the poem, Peter's resolve grew stronger, and with it a subtle awareness that he was involved in something bigger than the here and now.

It had begun years ago with his grandfather's interest in astronomy, which he had passed on to Peter, and with it his attraction to the Pleiades. There were hints along the way indicating Peter's connection to Olaquecha and his past life as Padura: his boyhood dreams of seeing the Pleiades upside down, as they appear in the Andean sky, which he realized the first time he saw them overhead during his healing ceremony; his uncanny ability to tell the time by reading the sun's position in the sky, which he had learned during Padura's boyhood; and his firm belief that Attu's vision to heal the reincarnate of Padura was from a higher intelligence—a god, or an entity, or some unexplainable essence of higher being.

Now he was coming full circle, as though his life journey was on a track back to his life as Peter Richards. It came over him that for the last eight years, he had been sleepwalking through life, and now he was more than willing to risk this life as Padura to return home to his wife and son as Peter Richards.

But, if members of the rescue party died in this endeavor, along with him, then what? There were the lives of five good men to consider, including his son, who had his entire life in front of him.

What would happen to their loved ones on news of their demise, or possibly no news? Debra, as strong and as good a woman she was, would never recover if Devon did not return home. *The horror of the shade.*

On the other hand, the five good men were determined to take Peter back down the mountain. Yachay and Tian were adamant about breaking the curse and returning to the village that they rightfully belonged in. Bob had lived a life that most people didn't experience in five lifetimes, and he was all in. Rudy wanted to honor his good friend Aldo and finish the job of guiding Peter down the mountain. That left Devon, twenty-two years of age. The look in Peter's son's eyes when at first he told him he couldn't leave the village was one of determined resistance, a look that screamed, *I will not leave here without you, Dad.*

So, Peter thought, as his mind coalesced, *we are all captains of our unconquerable soul.*

CHAPTER

24

A t dusk, the villagers were gathered around the bonfire
that sent crackling orange flames high into the sky, which
then died in a plush of violet, the stars emerging like little
portholes to the heavens.

For Tian, it felt right and proper to be back in the village with
his father at his side. Shortly after Tian's birth, Attu had expelled
his nephew, Yachay, from Olaquecha. But that did not deter Yachay
from covertly visiting his son under the cover of night.

Tian never knew when the nocturnal visits would come,
but despite only seeing his father a handful of times a year, an
inseparable bond formed. Tian's first memory of his father was
the sound of his voice whispering in his ear, "Y churi," (My son) as
Yachay nestled next to Tian in his bedroll, swallowing him up in
the warmth of his comforting embrace.

Tian could smell a mixture of strong scents exuding from his
father: the chill of the mountain mingled with the faint odor of
smoke clinging to his poncho; the familiar scent of his father's
sweat exuding from his pores, which always smelled so good to
Tian; and the smell of his curative remedies—a powdery, sweetish
smell.

When Tian was old enough, Yachay told compelling stories
of the history of the Quechua people, how out of a lake named
Titicaca, the god Viracocha emerged, bringing some human beings

with him. Then Viracocha created the Inti (sun), the moon, and the stars to light the world. He told of *The Wand* and *The Apparition of a Gloomy Path,* tales of betrayal and redemption. Yachay had learned these stories from his father, Havo, who, like his son and grandson, had lived outside their native village, surviving by their own wits and knowledge of the mountain.

By the age of ten, Tian was capable of going off on his own and meeting his father at various shelters down the mountain. When Tian was twelve, he and his father had built their mountainside grotto, where they kept the goats and llamas. By sixteen, tired of Attu's iron rule, Tian had left the village under his own volition, not waiting for Attu to expel him, like he did his father.

The death of Attu had brought the opportunity for Yachay and Tian to return to Olaquecha, but breaking the curse was imperative for a harmonious life, not only for Yachay and Tian but the entire village. Living under Attu had been prosperous at the table, for the food was plentiful, but bereft of the *sunqu* (heart). Tian, like every other member of the village, believed in the power of the curse. It must be broken. So, getting Padura down the mountain and away from the influence of Attu was necessary for all concerned. It was the only way for Tian to live the life he had imagined among his people, with his mother and father sharing the same roof for the rest of their lives.

When darkness came, the amber light from the fire showed the villagers like ghostly shadows. There was a murmur of anticipation among the people as Rumi stood before them, raising his hands for silence. "Attu told me on his deathbed," Rumi said, his hands thrust before him to emphasize the point, "that his wish was for me to become leader of the village."

Another murmur erupted from the people, a strained kind of sound, as if fearful of the impact of the words they were hearing.

Tian thought Rumi a weak little man not only in stature but also in his ability to think on his own. *The man has most likely never had an original idea,* Tian thought as Rumi extolled his qualification to lead the village. He said he had been at Attu's seat of power for so many years. "I will continue the reign of prosperity," he said in an overly loud voice, as though trying to convince himself and his listeners.

The people were getting restless, whispering among themselves. Tian heard Padura's name float like a flittering butterfly through the crowd.

At last, Rumi finished, slinking off into the shadows. As Padura came before the people, a deafening silence fell over the village; in the silence of the mountain, there is much you can learn.

"I have lived among you for eight years, and over that time, I have learned much about the journey of my spirit. I believe with all my heart that I am the reincarnate of Padura."

"Yah," the crowd said in a surge of emotion.

"But," Padura said with a lift of his hand, palms toward his audience, "in *this* life, I am Peter Richards." He pointed toward his son, Devon. "I have a son who came with these brave men." He extended his hand to the others standing next to Devon. "They have risked everything to take me back to my wife in America." Padura paused as a swell of emotion rose in his throat. "For all these years, I have resisted leaving for fear not of what would become of me but of those who helped me."

Padura brought his hands together, fingers laced. "My comrades," Padura said with an opening of his hand toward Tian and the others, "are convinced that by leaving this mountain, Attu's curse will be broken."

"Mana!" (No!) Rumi shouted in a shrill voice.

Padura turned his attention to the stooped, shadowy figure. "Attu saved my life, and for that I am forever grateful, Rumi." Peter turned back to the villagers, hands spread out to his side. "But Attu was a selfish man, a bad man, who did what was only best for Attu and the accumulation of power. Everyone gathered here knows it is true."

Rumi started to speak, and Padura raised his hand for him to stop.

"It is best for all of us if I leave the village and by doing so break Attu's curse."

"Who will lead us if you leave us, Padura?" a villager said in a fretful tone.

The man went on to say that he feared for the well-being of the crops and the health of the villagers without his presence. "Yah," the voices said.

Yachay stepped forward and spoke in a clear, strong voice. There was a musical quality to his words that Tian found inspiring.

Yachay said that Padura had paid his dues to the village. "We thank you greatly," he said with a nod toward Padura, "but now it is time for you to go back to your world, and Tian and I to live back in ours."

There was much back and forth between Yachay and Tian and the villagers. Rumi remained silent.

Padura came up next to Yachay and put his arm on his shoulder. "This is a good man, an intelligent man, who knows the ways of this mountain inside and out." Padura squeezed Yachay's shoulder and nodded his approval. "Yachay should be the new tribal chief." He told the gathering that he was the rightful heir as the son of Havo, whom Attu had conspired against. His and Tian's presence would ensure harmony. "Yachay allin Kamachiq." (Yachay good leader.)

As a murmur rose through the people like a rising tide, Padura stepped back into the crowd but not before raising his hand to Rumi, indicating to hear Yachay out. Yachay said that for his deputy, he needed a man with experience in the ways of the village and a man he could lean on for advice. He asked Rumi if he would accept his offer.

All eyes were on the Rumi, who shook his head. "No. No. No." He said he was the rightful heir, and if Peter departed, the curse would wreak havoc on all of them on their way down the mountain. With raised fist, he said, "Qam muna rikai pay shaman's luqhiyay." (You shall see the shaman's wrath.)

A hum grew among the villagers like a hornet's nest. "Rumi mana allin," the voices said. (Rumi bad man.)

Rumi looked into a sea of unified people, their eyes taut and honed in on him. He raised his hands for silence. He looked off for a moment. His eyes, previously two angry slits, were now open and acquiescing. He seemed to realize he had only one option. "Ñuqa añikuy." (I accept.)

CHAPTER

25

A celebration was organized to celebrate the new leader and to wish Padura a safe journey. A stronger, alcoholic version of chicha was broken out that had the menfolk feeling no pain. Over the course of the evening, two or three men would approach Devon's father, standing in front of his hut. Heads would bow, accompanied by grateful smiles. "Ñoqanchis agradisikuyki, Padura." (We thank you, Padura.)

Devon noticed his father's comfort with these short brown men and the easy manner in which he listened attentively, a hand on the shoulder, an appreciative smile. He also noticed, or sensed, a vibration of energy emanating from his father—as though preparing for battle not of the body but of the mind, Padura versus the spirit of Attu, the evil conjurer.

After the last of the villagers had thanked Peter, he joined Devon, Bob, and Rudy at a table at the cooking hut, sitting in front of empty bowls and platters of goat stew and cooked potatoes, boiled quinoa, and oca.

Mariaqua brought a plate of food to Peter. He thanked her and told his tablemates that Yachay and Tian had decided that Yachay should stay at the village. "It would not look good if he were to depart his first day in office. I think Rumi realizes his place in the village is now secure, but I wouldn't trust him initially."

It was a great relief for Devon to have his father heading out with them in the morning, but he had a nagging feeling that they were not out of the woods yet. There was a cloud of anticipation hanging over the table, a mood of confident determination with a wariness of apprehension.

After Peter finished eating, Devon, Bob, and Rudy went with Peter to his hut, and Tian and Yachay went to Mariaqua's, a family once again.

As tired as Devon was, sleep did not come easily. A jangled excitement coursed through his body as he lay between his father and Bob, both sound asleep, as was Rudy, who was gently snoring. Outside, the celebration was ending with an occasional fading rumble of laughter and murmur of conversation.

Devon tried to block out thoughts of the journey ahead to bring his father home and then the emotion of his mother upon seeing both of her men back. But he had an ominous sense that getting down the mountain all in one piece was going to be a challenge. He wasn't sure if it was the curse or some other intuition.

CHAPTER

26

At dawn, they ate at the cooking hut, served by Mariaqua. Yachay then walked them over to the trailhead. He hugged Tian and then offered his hands, which the others clasped in a circle. "Ñuqayku sinchi," they said with one voice.

Past the llama pasture, the trail wound around a series of boulders, which reminded Devon of sentries guarding the secrets of the village of Olaquecha. The morning air was foggy and brisk with a feel of moisture to it. Tian and Bob walked point, Devon and Peter behind, and Rudy pulling up the rear.

Walking down the mountain was not as strenuous, though it did put pressure on Devon's knees. From time to time, he checked on his father, whose stride was sure and strong, but his demeanor was tense, as though he was preparing for the worst.

By midmorning, snow had begun to fall, a light, fluffy snow that offered little impediment. Around a bend, the fog thickened so that their visibility was only a few yards. Devon was glad that Tian was leading them, for last night his father had told him that Tian knew these trails like the back of his hand.

Along with the low visibility, the snow increased with a swirling wind.

Through a steep-sided gully, they came to a halt at the edge of the meadow of wildflowers surrounded by walls of rock, where Bob had told them to go on without him. The mountains in the distance, covered by a shroud of fog, were not visible. Nor were the wildflowers now covered in snow.

Rudy and Tian conferred. "We are a couple of hours from the ruins," Rudy said. "Tian says we should hunker down there for a meal and then see."

"Allin," Peter said.

As they trudged through the snow, now up to their ankles, Devon wondered if the challenges ahead would be more mental than physical, a psychological battle of mind over matter.

From the trail, the ruins looked different under a layer of powdery white. The intricate workmanship of the walls and structures was hidden, as were the steps that they carefully descended. The pointy-topped rock formations at the edge of the promontory were now an opaque blur of bumps.

They ate quinoa and flatbread in the opening in the side of the mountain where they had previously slept. They were quiet during the meal, with an occasional glance outside at the fog and snow.

Tian spoke to Rudy, who said, "Tian thinks it best if we stay here until morning."

Tian lifted his chin toward the outside. "Mana allin." (No good.)

Peter's gaze, a mixture of derring-do and apprehension, was fixed intently on his son. "Good," he said, turning his attention to the misty snow steadily falling from the sky.

For the remainder of the afternoon, they lounged inside the grotto, Rudy taking a siesta inside his sleeping bag, Tian, sitting against the back wall, lost in thought with an occasional glance outside as the snow continued. The three Americans were mostly silent, as though taking their mind off anything other than getting down the mountain was a distraction.

There were many things Devon wanted to discuss with his father about his time in Olaquecha, and also to tell him about his life from high school through college. And, of course, he wanted to talk about astronomy—when the next eclipse was—and about going to the observation deck when they got home. But all of that seemed as though it was testing fate. *Get down the mountain,* Devon thought, *and then we have the rest of our lives to talk and stargaze.*

By nightfall, the snow had stopped, but the air had turned windy and cold. The alcove offered relief from the wind, and Devon bundled himself into his sleeping bag. Physically, he was fine, but the mental aspect was beginning to wear on him—a fear of what lay ahead, of what challenges this mountain had in store for them. Devon had read Kafka in college, where the protagonist faced surrealistic predicaments.

He considered them continually walking around the mountain, fighting the elements and never escaping its hold on them.

His last thought before drifting off to sleep was of his father walking back up the mountain and looking over his shoulder at Devon. "Tell your mother I will always love her, but it is not to be."

By midmorning, they came to a patch of barren land littered with boulders. It looked out over a valley of scrub trees and rocks. The sun was peeking out from between the clouds, and the moisture had left the air, though it was still cold. They were moving at a good pace, and the light snow on the ground was no problem to traverse.

They wove their way through a narrow pass then down one steep trail and then another. Devon lost himself in the physical challenge, as his knees ached from the downward trek. He kept his eyes open for the unexpected—a rockslide? He felt anything possible in this unforgiving land.

The goal for the day was to make it to Tian's mountain hut. It would seem a victory to spend their second night in relative comfort. The other members of the party all seemed good. Tian and Rudy, Devon never considered a worry; they were in their element, especially Tian. But Bob and he were mana riqsisqa in this land of sky and mountain, and at any moment, their bodies could fail them.

As for his father, Devon wasn't sure what to expect. Yes, he had lived in this environment for the last eight years, but Peter Richards was a wild card. Devon was still a bit uncertain about his mental health and well-being. When he had first seen his father in the village, Peter Richards had fainted at the sight of Devon. It hinted at more than the shock of seeing his son, but also the duress of enduring an existence away from his loved ones. If they met adversity, would Peter want to return, not wanting to risk their lives?

During the reciting of the poem, with each stanza, Peter's voice had grown stronger and more confident, but that was then, the powerful words having taken hold of his father. But now, out in the elements, would those words begin to waver? Would Devon's father have second thoughts? Yesterday, during the swirling snow, Peter's expression had an *oh-oh* look that said, *I have experienced this before, and it is not good.* And later in the alcove, Devon saw conflict in his father's eyes. He had never seen such uncertainty hanging over his dad, who had always been confident in any situation.

They came to the stretch of barren land that looked out over the rocky valley of scrub trees, now dusted by a misty blanket of white. Their visibility of the immediate area was manageable, but the mountains in the distance had faded behind the gray sky that seemed to be closing in, ready to swallow everything.

One foot after another, they continued down the mountain. It all seemed so different from the climb up. Now, everyone seemed on the lookout—a glance here, a glance there.

On and on they trekked down the mountain, stopping only twice for water breaks. As the last of daylight was fading, they came to halt on the rise overlooking a snow-covered clearing, the llama corral.

"What a sight for these old tired eyes," Bob said. "What do you think, Peter?" he said with a lift in his voice.

"Never thought I'd ..." Peter caught himself, as though he were pushing his luck. He lifted his chin, indicating to continue walking.

Tian's hut offered immediate warmth, the mountainside providing good insulation from the elements.

After storing their backpacks, Rudy told the Americans to stay inside and rest while he and Tian tended to the goats and llamas and started a fire for dinner. "Please," Rudy said, anticipating an argument, "save your strength for tomorrow."

Scrunched around the table, they ate boiled quinoa, flatbread, and warmed jerky. There had been little conversation since departing, and the meal was the same, other than Rudy and Tian discussing the trek for the next day.

"The recess in the gully," Rudy said, "where we spent the night is our goal for tomorrow."

They were drinking chicha tea at the table. Peter and Bob sat in the chairs made of wood and vines, the others on sacks of grain. "One day at a time," Bob said with a lift of his brow. He looked at Peter, who sat across from Bob with a blank-faced expression, almost as though he were in a trance.

"Dad?" Devon said.

Peter looked at his son and then the rest of the table. A cloud seemed to come over his eyes. "One day at a time," Peter said in a sullen, robotic voice.

CHAPTER

27

Bob was worried about Peter, not only about his seemingly depressed mental state but also his dry, scratchy cough. It started after they turned in the previous night and lasted for a couple of minutes before a reprieve, and then after anywhere from a few minutes to an hour, it started again.

At first light, Bob went over to Peter, who was lying on his back in his sleeping bag. Peter's eyes were wide open, his face a blank slate.

"Peter," Bob said. "How are you feeling?"

"I can't feel my legs," Peter said through a gasping cough.

Devon came over to Peter's side. He started to speak, then hesitated and looked at Bob.

Bob checked Peter over and found no signs of illness. His throat was clear, and his pulse was strong. Everything looked good.

Tian handed Bob a spoonful of the godawful green liquid that he had taken for altitude sickness.

Tian lifted his chin, indicating for the doctor to give it to Peter.

Peter swallowed the medicine and then gasped and coughed.

It almost seemed to Bob as though, dare he think it, the curse was engulfing Peter.

"We have to get my dad off this mountain," Devon said.

"Attu ..." Peter said in a faint voice, "came to me in a dream last night." Peter asked for water, and Devon got his canteen and gave

137

his father a sip. "I am *llulla*, a traitor for deserting Olaquecha. The shaman intends to not let me get off this mountain alive."

"No," Tian said with power, like a locomotive picking up steam. He reached for Peter's hand and extended his other hand to Devon, who took Rudy's, who took Bob's, who took Peter's. Tian leaned into Peter so that their faces were inches apart. "Ñuqayku sinchi," Tian said in a low voice. "Ñuqayku sinchi," he said in a stronger voice.

Tian looked around at the others and then Peter. "Ñuqayku sinchi," they said in unison.

Tian retrieved a travois from under a shelter in the corral. He and Rudy secured Peter on the travois platform of leather netting with straps. They secured a leather harness across their chests, like a pair of draft horses. Each man then grabbed a pole in the front and dragged Peter outside. The snow provided good traction, and with two capable men pulling, they headed out around the corral.

The air was dry, and the sun was rising over a pristine clear sky. Perfect conditions, save the patient. Bob wondered if Peter had psyched himself into temporary paralysis. Normally, a patient with a cough like Peter's would have swollen glands or a raw throat. Could the cough also be psychosomatic?

Past the llama corral, they swished through the long meadow now blanketed in white.

The feathery snow was not much of an impediment. Through the rocky-walled opening, they passed the lake.

Rudy and Tian seemed to be holding up well as they came to a halt at the first of the switchback trails. Peter was lying back, his head in front, with his hands at his side, still with that trancelike expression.

"We must all be careful on these switchbacks," Rudy said as he and Tian began down the mountain.

Bob asked if they should rotate on the travois. "No," Rudy said. "We are good." Rudy looked at Tian, who glanced back at Peter and nodded as if to say, *We have this, amigo.*

After completing the switchbacks, they arrived at a level area. Below were the brown valley floor and the silver stream that ran near the hut, where Bob could barely make out Rudy's car, a small, dark speck on the brown landscape. It seemed so close yet so far, another world from the one he stood in.

The snow was only in spots now in this lower elevation, but it didn't seem to bother Rudy and Tian as they continued downward. Tian had mentioned last night that Yachay had rescued Peter with the same travois, though up the mountain and by himself, from the bridge to his mountainside hut—amazing.

When they arrived at the gorge, they were in for a shock: the swinging maguey bridge spanned across to the other side. "How is that possible?" Devon said.

Peter turned his head and looked hard at the bridge. "It is a trap. Do *not* cross it."

Rudy questioned Tian, who said he didn't know how the bridge had been built, especially in such a short amount of time.

"What do you think, Rudy?" Bob said.

Rudy placed one foot on the edge of the bridge and grabbed the vine handrail. He shook the bridge. "It seems very sturdy."

"I will not allow anyone to cross that bridge," Peter croaked in a hoarse voice. He had coughed sporadically on the trek down but nothing like last night.

Tian said something to Peter. "Tian agrees." Peter looked at the others. "Are we all in agreement?"

"Yes," Rudy said.

Bob nodded. "I've seen enough to not want to tempt that bridge."

"Me too," Devon added.

Without warning, a strong gale-like wind—like a wind tunnel— swept through the gorge, shaking the bridge. Then came a ghostly, hollow roar echoing off the canyon walls. The bridge swayed wildly, creaking like a coffin door closing. A crack like a rifle shot, and then on the far end, a timber truss began to lose its hold of the mountainside. The trusses broke away, and with that, the bridge swung out like a trapeze, flapping wildly against the canyon wall.

As suddenly as it had begun, the wind died down, the bridge now looking exactly like when they had found it on the way up the mountain, the stringy remains of the bridge of vines hanging down from the other side, once again bringing to mind a hangman's noose. Bob thought of the Shakespeare quote: "There are more things in heaven and earth, Horatio, than are dreamt of in your philosophy."

CHAPTER

28

They slowed down as they zigzagged down the hillside of the gorge. Rudy and Tian were careful in maneuvering the travois on this short, windy trail. As the trail leveled off, they picked up speed, meandering down the gorge.

Peter felt so helpless having Rudy and Tian traverse him down the mountain. He also felt anxious as to what may lie ahead.

The signs were all so frighteningly similar to when Peter and Aldo had descended the mountain: the unpredictable swirling snow, the gloomy sense that they were fighting an all-powerful, all-knowing force—which Peter believed had caused his immobile state—and then the collapse of the swinging bridge of maguey plants, which immediately brought to mind Aldo falling three hundred feet, thudding face-first onto a large rock, dead. Peter had stood on the cliff edge stunned, trembling as the wind disappeared as quickly as it had arrived, his entire body shaking. When the bridge collapsed the second time, a shuddering surge of anxiety, a déjà vu sense, overcame his being.

But there was no turning back, and descending the mountain was the only choice, though he feared greatly that calamity was in their future—the others perishing one by one, leaving him alone. Attu would then come to him in the most horrible of nightmares. "I have not only taken the lives of your friends, Padura, but that of your son. You will never leave this mountain. Never!"

At that point, death would be a relief. Even if he somehow managed to escape the mountain, how could he possibly return home and tell Debra that he had survived but that their son was dead? Or tell Bob's wife, Carey, that her husband of more than forty years was dead? Or contact Rudy's family? And when Tian did not return to the village, Yachay would go out and search and discover his son's remains.

Continuing down the mountain, Peter looked up and checked the sun sitting high and strong in the western sky. He figured they had approximately three more hours of sunlight. He thought it possible they could make it to the recess before nightfall. Before going to Olaquecha, Peter had taken for granted his uncanny ability to tell the time by reading the sun's position in the sky, able to tell how much sunlight they had left within a minute or two. On his fateful trek down the mountain with Aldo, he had lost that ability, an eerie, unsettling warning of things to come.

When they came to a clearing of wild grass and rubble, Bob asked if they could stop.

"How do your legs feel, Peter?" He hadn't coughed since they left the remains of the bridge.

Peter looked quizzically at Bob. He extended his hand, and Bob helped him to his feet. "No good," Peter said.

"Dad?"

"Dev," Peter said as he settled back on the travois, "let's just keep moving."

Peter turned to his carriers. "Allin?"

Rudy and Tian exchanged a quick look, a look that said, *We can take you all the way down this mountain if need be.*

Peter was impressed with the manner in which these two Peruvian men handled every situation. There was a quiet confidence about them. There was nothing on this mountain that together they couldn't conquer, curse or no curse. Their confidence offered Peter reassurance that he was in good hands.

By the time they reached the recess, dusk was settling over the land. They sat in a circle, eating flatbread and jerky. There remained a sense of doom hanging in the air. All that they had witnessed today was something to behold.

Bob had a look on his face that Peter knew. It was a look of one who had witnessed things beyond the world from which he came. At horseshoes, he had told Peter about stories he had heard in faraway lands of the mysteries of indigenous cultures, but this was Dr. Goodman's first time witnessing the unexplainable. How did the bridge get built? Where did the wind come from that destroyed the bridge? How did Peter lose the use of his legs?

Even after what they had witnessed today, Peter could see a glimmer of confidence in the eyes of the good doctor, though with a dose of wariness in the downward slant at the corners. It was a look that said, *We must be vigilant, but in two days, we could be driving away.*

But Peter knew that two days on this mountain could be an eternity.

CHAPTER

29

When they reached the stepping-stones to cross the creek, it was midmorning. Upstream and around a bend, hidden from sight, would be the remains of the swinging bridge. Yesterday had been a day Devon would remember in detail for the rest of his life. The events were hard to digest—his father unable to walk, the bridge spanning across the gorge, and then its terrifying destruction.

Even with all that, Devon had slept reasonably well last night, but he was awoken a couple of times by his father thrashing about in his sleeping bag, talking to himself in hurried, frightened breaths. "No, Attu, no!"

But each step they took got them one step closer to escape. Yes, that is what it seemed to Devon—escape. As he stood on the other side of the creek, waiting for Tian and Rudy to shoulder his father across, he felt as though they were leaving the scene of a crime. Aldo Coreas had lost his life falling into these waters.

As they began the ascent up the other side of the gorge, Devon would be relieved when the creek was out sight. The goal for today was to reach the stone huts where they had first met Yachay. Only a few days had passed since then, but it seemed so very long ago.

By noon, they had reached the top of the gorge, and Devon took one last look over his shoulder. It was a hauntingly beautiful sight from high above. Sunlight glinted on the water, the golden-ocher canyon walls rose on both sides of the stream, and the snowcapped mountains in the distance overlooked it all like mountain deities.

"Let us eat up ahead," Rudy said as he lifted his chin toward a meadow of scrub and rubble.

As usual, they sat in a circle, eating in silence. But the group all seemed in reasonably good shape—save his father's temporary paralysis, though Devon did wonder how much longer Rudy and Tian could continue pulling Peter in the travois. But the two of them worked in perfect unison, like dance partners who knew the other's move before it was made, seemingly unaware of the physical difficulty of such a feat.

Devon would not relax in regard to his father until they were off this mountain. Even in his immobile situation, his dad looked as though he had hardly aged. His hair, long and full, had only a few traces of gray. His mahogany beard, flecked with gray, was rather light in fullness but contrasted with his ruddy cheeks. He looked like a handsome, fit hippy, but a hippy with a serious concern burning in his eyes.

It was tacitly understood by all that Devon's father was going through some type of withdrawal from all that he had endured. Having Bob, Rudy, and Tian along was a great asset. One was a very wise physician, another a skilled guide, and then Tian, who was like the soul of this mountain, a man whom Devon considered a huge asset in combating the curse. He wondered if someday Tian wouldn't become the shaman in Olaquecha. He seemed to be in tune with the rhythms of this land, as if he had an inner antenna tuned to the mountain's frequency.

As they stood and slipped on their backpacks, Rudy handed out coca and lime, and off they went.

The trail led down through a rocky gully. They were in a downward descent, and Devon noticed his breathing was easier at the lower altitude. But his body was one big sore muscle, and he wondered how Bob was holding up. The good doctor seemed okay physically as he walked next to him. Ahead of Devon were Rudy and Tian, pulling his father in the travois.

Past the gully, Tian pointed to his left. It dawned on Devon that this was not the way they had come; in fact, they had been on a different route since shortly after they had crossed the creek. He assumed it must be a route more conducive to pulling the travois.

The trail, bordered by rocks and boulders of all sizes, was plenty wide enough for two men to walk side by side. The sky overhead was crystal blue, the air dry, and the temperature brisk but comfortable. Other than his father's situation, things were going smoothly. But Devon had a foreboding sense that the curse had more in store for them.

The trail led down to a level stretch. To their left was a meadow of deep-purple and bright-yellow wildflowers, and on their right was a rocky hillside, with massive stones embedded in the hill and gnarly shrubs.

They stopped. Rudy went off to the side of the trail near the meadow, leaning his back against a big rock, and removed a pebble from his boot.

Tian raised his hand. He cocked his head, listening. "Qurriy," he shouted, waving the group forward. He grabbed both poles, pulling the travois as Peter held on for dear life.

Devon heard a low rumble like a mounting storm as the first rock tumbled down the hillside.

Rocks and boulders rumbled down, smashing over the small green shrubs. It seemed like the mountain was shrugging the boulders out of its surface.

Everything seemed to slow down as Devon and Bob raced forward, rocky debris crashing onto the trail all around them. Ahead, Tian was pulling Peter into an alcove in the side of the hill.

Devon and Bob rushed in to join them. No one was sure where Rudy was.

Tian unstrapped Peter from the travois and placed him in a sitting position against the back wall as the rocks crashed down onto the trail and into the meadow. There was dust everywhere as the tremendous rumbling roar of the landslide shook the ground they stood on. It sounded as though the mountain were coming apart.

The four men under cover waited for what seemed hours but was only a few minutes. When it ended, Tian stepped out, looked around, and then waved the all-safe sign. There were massive boulders and rocks of varying sizes scattered about the once pristine meadow. It looked like a geologist's junkyard.

Bob spotted Rudy's boot on the trail. "Rudy!" he yelled. "Rudy!"

Tian, Bob, and Devon began a frantic search, with Peter having crawled outside the opening, sitting on the trail and scanning the hillside for Rudy.

"I'm good, amigos," said a voice that seemed to be coming from the hill.

"Rudy, where are you?" Bob said as all eyes turned to the sound of his voice.

From behind a massive boulder at the base of the hill, Rudy emerged, crawling on his hands and knees through a narrow gap between the hill and the boulder. He stood, dusted himself off, and looked at his comrades with a crooked smile. "What is the saying in America?" he said as he walked toward his companions none the worse for wear. "If you can't beat them, join them." He took his boot from Bob as the others converged around him. Shoulders were slapped, hands clasped, and Tian and Rudy embraced.

"As I was about to run for it, I got a sudden cramp in my leg," Rudy said as he clutched his thigh. "I hobbled over to the hillside and placed myself between that big stone and the mountain." Rudy threw his hands in front of himself. "Those big boulders?" he said with a shake of his head. "They came without warning." He said something to Tian. "Tian says he heard the mountain whisper a warning."

"It's the curse," Peter said. "Devon." He waved his son over to him. "Help me stand up, son."

Peter asked Devon to turn him so that he faced the hillside, his arm over Devon's shoulder. Rudy came over to support him from the other side. There was a look in Devon's father's eyes that he hadn't seen since when he was a boy. It was a determined look of a man who was prepared to challenge the horror of the shade.

"Attu," Peter shouted. "Attu! You saved my life, and I will owe you for whatever time I have left. But I gave eight years of my life to you and your village as the incarnate of Padura. You are dead, and whether you like it or not, Yachay is the new leader, and he has asked me to return to my home. I will not return to the village."

Peter paused for a moment to catch his breath. "Kill me if you must. Kill all of us," he said, looking around for confirmation that was met by nods of approval. "But I will not return up this mountain. If you really care about Olaquecha, you will look kindly on your people, for it was under your leadership that Padura returned and stayed until your death. Your corporeal being has left Viracocha's land of sky and mountain." Peter raised his hand overhead, finger pointing toward the heavens. "It is my time to return to my world as Peter Richards. Allow us safe passage."

Peter raised his hand, indicating to wait a minute. He scrunched up his face, raising his brow.

It reminded Devon of when they would stargaze, and his father had just seen something amazing, like when they observed the waxing gibbous moon occulting the northern section of the Pleiades.

"I have feeling in my legs!" Peter said in a tone of disbelief. "I have feeling in my legs!"

Peter grabbed Devon's forearm and began to gingerly walk. He lifted one leg and then the other. "By God, I can walk."

A look of anticipation came over Peter Richards's face—a look that said, *I think we might make it.*

CHAPTER

30

Tian and Bob took the lead, followed by Devon and Peter, with Rudy in the rear. They continued on in silence, much as before, but Devon felt a guarded optimism that they would all make it out alive.

Through a deep-walled canyon, they continued the downward trek. Devon was physically tired and worn. After his father's tirade at Attu and then his ability to walk again, Devon felt a sense of relief, but with it came a bone-weary fatigue. His mind and body had been in a tight and tense state, and now he was walking on fumes.

His father, on the other hand, seemed to be walking with a purpose, his gaze straight ahead, his square shoulders straight and true, reminding Devon of when they would trek through a park, up and down rolling hills and forest glens, to find a secluded spot near a creek or stream.

They would set up camp and then, if there was still daylight, fish for their dinner. As the dusky sky darkened, the stars would emerge. Devon and his father would scan the sky with their binoculars; the sight of the stars sparkling like a cluster of jewels in the blue-black sky created a bond between young Devon Richards and his father. "Dad, Dad," young Devon had said in a tone of discovery on their first camping trip, "I see Ursa Major."

Devon knew he shouldn't get ahead of himself, but he had a question for his father after the evening meal.

In the late afternoon, they came to the stone ruins. The sight of the promontory jutting out of the side of the mountain held Devon's gaze for a moment. *That would make a good spot,* he thought. They dropped their backpacks on a large, flat stone in the middle of the ruins. Off to their left, the stone huts dotting the cliff looked like a four-star luxury hotel.

"Let us collect firewood and water," Rudy said as he looked up toward the trail, across which was the rocky scree and gnarly trees.

"Rudy," Bob said, "let Devon, Peter, and I collect the firewood." Bob looked at Rudy and then Tian. "A small thank-you."

Rudy flashed a sly grin at Tian, who smiled handsomely, his strong white teeth seeming to sparkle in the late-afternoon light.

"Thank you," Rudy said. "We accept."

The three men walked past the columns of massive recessed stones, where human sacrifices had been performed centuries ago, up the steps, across trail and the shingly scree.

They walked past the gnarled trees growing in the earth and between fissures in the rock to the pool of water surrounded by sharp crested ridges and finger-shaped stones. Peter looked at the water trickling down the face of a rocky cliff directly across from where they stood. "It was here," Peter said in a low voice, a voice filled with reverence, "that Yachay told me I was on a journey with the great spirit of the mountain."

Peter bent down, cupped a handful of water, and drank. He stood and said, "And now that journey is coming to an end." He looked up into the sky and shielded his eyes from the sun, his squinty expression one Devon hadn't seen since their last camping trip together. "By my calculation, it is 4:07."

Bob checked his watch on his wrist and offered a huge grin. "On the money, Peter. On. The. Money." Bob placed his hand on Peter's shoulder. "It's good to have you back, old friend."

By dusk, the food had been eaten, mostly in silence, as though it would not be wise to test fate. Pointing to the edge of the promontory, Devon said to Peter, "Dad, what say we walk over and stargaze with the naked eye?"

Peter looked around the circle of men, as though trying to gauge an opinion.

"That sounds like a grand idea," Bob said.

Rudy said, "Tian would like to join you."

"Everyone," Peter said, standing.

From the edge of the peninsula, Devon looked out at the mountains strung across the horizon like dark, blurry mounds in the fading light. Below, he could barely make out a stream running through a smattering of trees lining the shoreline.

"Look, Dad," Devon said, pointing to the western sky. "Venus."

"Yes," Peter said with a rise of enthusiasm. "The evening star, shining so bright."

"To its left is Jupiter," Bob said.

"Yah," Tian said. He spoke to Rudy and then said, "He says it is a good sign to see Venus and Jupiter so close together and shining so bright."

They stood watching as though mesmerized as the two stars began to slowly dip into the horizon.

Peter turned around and focused on the eastern sky. He pointed to a twinkling red star. "Mars. Hello, neighbor."

Peter then turned back toward the valley as though sensing something. He pointed to a dark speck circling high overhead. As it neared, its size became evident. It was a huge bird.

"El condor," Tian said.

The bird soared, circling a swath of air, rising and falling with the currents. It flapped it massive wings once and soared off, disappearing into the darkness.

Tian said, "El condor, huq kutikama, Padura." (El Condor says goodbye, Padura.)

Rudy hurried off and returned with his flute, then handed it to Tian, who began to play. His haunting music was a blend of joy and sadness, a song of life. He played facing the mountains as the last violet flush of sunlight faded away.

CHAPTER

31

The final walk down the mountain seemed like a carefree stroll to Devon. Yes, his body was achingly sore, but his rising spirit could no longer be denied. His companions too all walked with an extra giddyap in their step.

Midday, they came to the terraced section of rocky steps that led down to an obelisk of stones. The stones were in a field of wildflowers that overlooked the valley where they had stopped on the first day up the mountain.

They ate the same meal of bread and raw quinoa but this time with an undeniable attitude of certainty. They still remained mostly silent, though Devon thought it might be more from fatigue at this point than any fear of testing fate.

Of course, Rudy and Tian appeared capable of walking for days without a problem, but Bob had a general look of being tuckered out. He slowly chewed his food as though the act was a great effort. His eyes had the glazed-over look of someone who had been through a great ordeal.

Devon's father also looked worn out but with an open-eyed look of someone embarking on a new phase of his life, a new beginning.

All in all, they were good. Last night's stargazing was a special night that Devon would never forget, especially after they saw el condor. After dusk, the sky had been clear, and the full moon lit up the valley in a ray of silver light. They spotted the Little and Big

Dippers and a cluster of stars that had been near and dear to Peter Richards since childhood.

"There," Peter said, pointing.

"Maia," Tian said.

"The Pleiades," Rudy said, "are a major influence in Quechua culture. It is the home of Viracocha."

"From whence came Padura," Peter said with a confirming nod. "When we get home, I will tell you all about it, Dev." Peter smiled, mostly to himself. "Not sure you will believe it all, but ..." He shrugged as if to say, *It is what it is.*

By the time they got to the trailhead, Devon could see their starting point: the stream speckled with stones along its shore, the adobe hut with thatched roof, and Rudy's SUV. Never had a car looked so good.

"Allin samiyuq kay," Tian said, with his hand raised to say goodbye.

Everyone shook hands and exchanged hugs with Tian, Devon thanking him with broken Quechua. "Allin ..." Devon said, trying to remember the word for *journey*.

Tian smiled his magnificent smile.

Peter then embraced him and said in Tian's ear. "Agradisikuyki allin wawqi." (Thank you, good friend.)

They stood at the trailhead and watched as Tian began his journey back up the mountain. They stayed until he disappeared from sight.

Devon and his father sat in the back seat of Rudy's car, both insisting that Bob, with his long legs, sit up front.

They drove off, banging and bumping along over the rocky, rutted ground, parallel to the stream speckled with boulders and stones bordering its shoreline. Devon looked over his shoulder at the giant mountain named Olaquecha.

At last, he felt safe. At last, he looked at his father, and in that moment, as though it became apparent they were really safe, father and son embraced. "We made it, Dad," Devon said as the emotion rose in his throat, all of the worry and strain leaving his corporeal being.

"I love you, boy," Peter said with a catch in his throat.

When they exited the valley floor and drove on to the highway, Peter looked out his window. "People of the clouds," he said with hand raised. "Goodbye."

Printed in the United States
By Bookmasters